MUSIC OF THE INDIANS OF BRITISH COLUMBIA

Da Capo Press Music Reprint Series

MUSIC OF THE INDIANS OF BRITISH COLUMBIA

By Frances Densmore

DA CAPO PRESS · NEW YORK · 1972

Library of Congress Cataloging in Publication Data

Densmore, Frances, 1867-1957.
  Music of the Indians of British Columbia.

  (Da Capo Press music reprint series)
  Reprint of the 1943 ed., which was issued as
Anthropological paper 27 of the Bureau of American
Ethnology, p. 1-99 of its Bulletin 136.
  Bibliography: p.
  1. Indians of North America—Music. 2. Indians of
North America—British Columbia. I. Title.
II. Series: U.S. Bureau of American
Ethnology. Anthropological papers, 27.
ML3557.D3587   784.7'51   72-1879
ISBN 0-306-70507-9

This Da Capo Press edition of *Music of the Indians of
British Columbia* is an unabridged republication of
Anthropological Paper 27 of the Bureau of American
Ethnology, Smithsonian Institution, published originally
in Washington, D.C., in 1943 as pages 1-99 of Bulletin
136 of the Bureau of American Ethnology.

Published by Da Capo Press, Inc.
A Subsidiary of Plenum Publishing Corporation
227 West 17th Street, New York, New York 10011

MUSIC OF THE INDIANS
OF BRITISH COLUMBIA

SMITHSONIAN INSTITUTION
BUREAU OF AMERICAN ETHNOLOGY

Music of the Indians of British Columbia

By FRANCES DENSMORE

Anthropological Papers, No. 27

From Bureau of American Ethnology BULLETIN 136, pp. 1–99, pls. 1–9

UNITED STATES
GOVERNMENT PRINTING OFFICE
WASHINGTON : 1943

SMITHSONIAN INSTITUTION
Bureau of American Ethnology
Bulletin 136

Anthropological Papers, No. 27

Music of the Indians of British Columbia

By FRANCES DENSMORE

FOREWORD

Many tribes and locations are represented in the present work, differing from the writer's former books,[1] which have generally considered the music of only one tribe. This material from widely separated regions was available at Chilliwack, British Columbia, during the season of hop-picking, the Indians being employed in the fields. The work was made possible by the courtesy of Canadian officials. Grateful acknowledgment is made to Dr. Duncan Campbell Scott, Deputy Superintendent General, Department of Indian Affairs at Ottawa, who provided a letter of credential, and to Mr. C. C. Perry, Indian agent at Vancouver, and Indian Commissioner A. O. N. Daunt, Indian agent at New Westminster, who extended assistance and cooperation. Acknowledgment is also made of the courtesy of Walter Withers, corporal (later sergeant), Royal Canadian Mounted Police, who acted as escort between Chilliwack and the hop camp, and assisted the work in many ways. Courtesies were also extended by municipal officers in Chilliwack and by the executive office of the Columbia Hop Co., in whose camp the work was conducted.

This is the writer's first musical work in Canada and the results are important as a basis of comparison between the songs of Canadian Indians and those of Indians residing in the United States.

On this trip the writer had the helpful companionship of her sister, Margaret Densmore.

---

[1] See bibliography (Densmore, 1910, 1913, 1918, 1922, 1923, 1926, 1928, 1929, 1929 a, 1929 b, 1932, 1932 a, 1936, 1937, 1938, 1939, 1942).

CONTENTS

ILLUSTRATIONS

PLATES

TEXT FIGURES

LIST OF SONGS

1. ARRANGED IN ORDER OF SERIAL NUMBERS

SONGS WITH TREATMENT OF THE SICK

1. Arranged in Order of Serial Numbers—Continued

Dance Songs

1. Arranged in Order of Serial Numbers—Continued

Love Songs

Divorce Songs

Miscellaneous Songs

2. Arranged in Order of Catalog Numbers

2. Arranged in Order of Catalog Numbers—Continued

Catalog No.	Title of song	Name of singer	Serial No.	Page
1683	Song to a spirit in the fire	Jane Green	85	86
1684	Divorce dance song (a)	____do	83	84
1685	Divorce dance song (b)	____do	84	85
1686	"Wrap a feather around me"	____do	73	77
1687	"I am going to stay at home"	____do	80	82
1688	"She is glad to see him"	Ellen Stevens	81	83
1689	"Give me a bottle of rum"	____do	82	83
1690	Dance song from Babine	Abraham Williams	47	58
1691	"I am going to cure this sick man"	F. Knightum	11	30
1692	"The thunderbird will help me cure this sick man."	____do	14	32
1693	"I am trying to cure this sick man"	____do	12	31
1694	"The whale is going to help me cure this sick man."	____do	13	32
1695	Song of Y'ak, the medicine man (a)	____do	15	33
1696	Song of a medicine man at Nitinat Lake (a).	____do	23	39
1697	Song of a medicine man at Nitinat Lake (b).	____do	24	40
1698	Song of a medicine man at Carmanah	____do	26	41
1699	Song when going to war	____do	27	42
1700	Song when returning from war	____do	28	43
1701	War dance song	____do	29	44
1702	Song when carrying heads of the enemy on poles (a).	____do	30	45
1703	Song when carrying heads of the enemy on poles (b).	____do	31	46
1704	Dance song (a)	Annie Tom	40	54
1705	Dance song (b)	____do	41	54
1706	Klokali dance song	____do	44	56
1707	Song after receiving a gift (a)	____do	53	62
1708	Song after receiving a gift (b)	____do	54	62
1709	"I will scrape my body on the rocks"	____do	74	78
1710	Potlatch song	____do	36	50
1711	"I am going to make you better"	____do	19	36
1712	Song of dance with wolf headdress (a)	____do	50	60
1713	Song of dance with wolf headdress (b)	____do	51	60
1714	Song to a little girl	____do	76	80
1715	Song of Y'ak the medicine man (b)	Wilson Williams	16	34
1716	Song of Y'ak the medicine man (c)	____do	17	35
1717	Thunderbird dance song	____do	45	57
1718	Song of dance with wolf headdress (b)	Katharine Charlie	52	61
1719	Doctor Jim's song	____do	25	40
2021	Song concerning the prophet Skilmaha	Jimmie O'Hammon	86	87
2022	Song of a man alone at home	____do	97	94
2023	Slahal game song (b)	____do	60	68
2024	Dance song (d)	____do	43	55
2025	Dream of going to Ottawa	____do	92	90

2. Arranged in Order of Catalog Number—Continued

Cat-alog No.	Title of song	Name of singer	Se-rial No.	Page
2026	"This song cheers me"	Jimmie O'Hammon	18	36
2027	Song with termination of mourning	_____do_____	87	87
2028	Slahal game song (a)	_____do_____	59	67
2029	Song of happiness	_____do_____	91	90
2030	Song of a hunter	_____do_____	90	89
2031	Introductory song with treatment of the sick.	Tasalt	1	19
2032	Song when treating smallpox	_____do_____	2	20
2033	Song when treating hemorrhage from the lungs.	_____do_____	5	23
2034	Song when treating pneumonia	_____do_____	6	23
2035	Song when treating fever	_____do_____	3	21
2036	Song when treating palsy	_____do_____	4	22
2037	A desire for clear weather	_____do_____	35	49
2038	Song of pleasure	_____do_____	66	72
2039	The rider on the kohaks	_____do_____	33	47
2040	Dance song of the Fraser River Indians (a).	Dennis Peters	37	52
2041	Dance song of the Fraser River Indians (b).	_____do_____	38	52
2042	Dance song of the Fraser River Indians (c).	_____do_____	39	53
2043	A woman's song	_____do_____	96	93
2044	"I wish I were a cloud"	_____do_____	78	81
2045	"All my sweethearts are gone except one".	_____do_____	79	81
2046	Song of approach to a potlatch	_____do_____	34	49
2047	Dance song (c)	_____do_____	42	55
2048	Two girls on a horse (a and b)	John Butcher	7	25
2049	"Look at this sick person"	_____do_____	8	26
2050	An appeal to certain animals	_____do_____	9	27
2051	An appeal to the deer	_____do_____	10	28
2052	Slahal game song (c)	Otter Billie	61	69
2053	Slahal game song (d)	_____do_____	62	69
2054	Slahal game song (e)	_____do_____	63	70
2055	Dance song of the Thompson River Indians (a).	Henry McCarthy	48	59
2056	Dance song of the Thompson River Indians (b).	_____do_____	49	59
2057	Slahal game song (f)	_____do_____	64	70
2058	Gambling song (a)	Annie Bolem	67	72
2059	Indian cowboy song	_____do_____	98	94
2060	"Your pretty hair"	Julia Malwer	95	92
2061	The little boy and the whale	Jake George	75	79
2062	Song of a shark hunter	Wilson Williams	89	88
2063	Gambling song (b)	Julia Charlie	68	73

NAMES OF SINGERS, NUMBER OF SONGS TRANSCRIBED, AND HOME OF SINGER

Name	Number of songs	Home
Bob George	13	Powell River on Sliamon Reserve.
F. Knightum	13	Carmanah, on Vancouver Island.
Annie Tom	11	Nitinat village, on Vancouver Island.
Jimmie O'Hammon	10	Squamish River.
Tasalt	9	Near Chilliwack, on Fraser River.
Dennis Peters	8	Hope, on Fraser River.
Jane Green	5	Skeena River.
John Butcher	4	Lytton, on Thompson River at junction with Fraser.
Wilson Williams	4	Carmanah, on Vancouver Island.
Otter Billie	3	Thompson River.
Henry McCarthy	3	Thompson River.
Sophie Wilson	3	Church House, on Homalko Reserve.
Annie Bolem	2	Boothroyd, on Frazer River.
Katharine Charlie	2	Vancouver Island.
Ellen Stevens	2	Nass River.
Julia Charlie	1	Thompson River.
Jake George	1	
Henry Haldane	1	Port Simpson.
Johnson	1	Port Simpson.
Julia Malwer	1	Sardis.
Abraham Williams	1	Babine region.
Total	98	

SPECIAL SIGNS USED IN TRANSCRIPTIONS OF SONGS

⌐⎺⎺⎺⎺¬ placed above a series of notes indicates that they constitute a rhythmic unit.

(· placed above a note shows that the tone was prolonged slightly beyond the indicated time.

12

MUSIC OF THE INDIANS OF BRITISH COLUMBIA

By FRANCES DENSMORE

INTRODUCTION

The Indians of British Columbia find employment in the seasonal industries of the region, many working in the canneries and hop-picking camps. About 1,000 Indians were living in such a camp near Chilliwack in September 1926, and from these Indians the material here presented was obtained. They came from widely separated localities, including Vancouver and Cooper Islands, the Sliamon and Homalko Reserves, on the west coast of British Columbia, the vicinities of Port Simpson, the regions adjacent to the Fraser, Thompson, Nass, and Skeena Rivers, and the Babine country. The Indians of the latter localities must travel a considerable distance to the railroad. Thus a singer from the Skeena River said that she traveled 5 hours by automobile to reach Hazelton, and a singer from the Babine region made the trip to Hazelton by pack horse, traveling with a friend, after manner of Indian boys. The Babine region takes its name from a river that flows through a lake of the same name. It is a sparsely settled region and mountainous. The Indians of all the northern region assemble at Prince Rupert, whence they are taken to Vancouver by steamer. There they are joined by groups from other localities and transported to Chilliwack by electric cars. The journey is under the auspices of the several hop companies, and constables are provided by the Indian Office in each district through which they pass.

Chilliwack is located on the Fraser River, 65 miles southeast of Vancouver. The climate in the valley is particularly favorable to the raising of hops, which constitute an important industry. The workers in the Columbia Hop Co.'s Camp are housed in cabins and communal houses arranged in streets (pl. 1, fig. 1). In the distance are seen the mountains which, at this point, mark the boundary between the United States and Canada. There was an early, cold rain while the work was in progress, and snow appeared on the tops of these mountains.

The cabins generally housed two families (pl. 1, fig. 2). The communal houses (pl. 2, fig. 1) had an open space in the center,

13

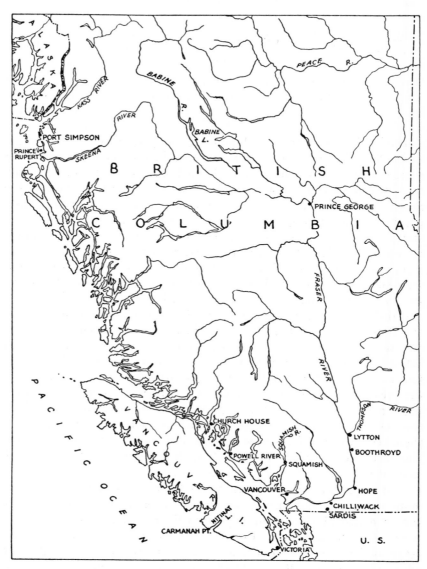

FIGURE 1.—Map of British Columbia.

extending the length of the building, with numerous cubicles on each side for separate families. Each cubicle had one window. The cooking was done on four or five stoves in the long central space, each family using the stove nearest its cubicle. The buildings and camp streets were lighted by electricity.

As the able-bodied people were at work during the day, it was necessary to record most of the songs in the evenings, and for this purpose the Hop Co. generously offered the use of a small building next the entrance that was used for Red Cross supplies and known as the Red Cross shack (pl. 2, fig. 2). This contained a small stove and had one small window on each of the sides not shown in the illustration. The shack was constructed of upright boards with wide cracks between them. When songs were being recorded, a crowd usually congregated outside the building and, as a reward for keeping quiet, they were allowed to look through the cracks, so that often a row of eyes could be seen through these perpendicular openings.

An interesting incident of a hop-picking camp is the exchange of articles of clothing brought for that purpose. The clothing of men, women, and children is exchanged in this manner, the transfers being attended by much discussion and bargaining, several garments often being exchanged for one of supposedly greater value. A group engaged in this form of barter is shown in plate 3, figure 1.

The harvesting of hops is a picturesque scene. Each vine climbs a cord which extends from the ground to a horizontal wire stretched between tall poles. A corner of a hop field is shown in plate 3, figure 2. When the hops are ripe these wires are lowered to permit the picking of the hops (pl. 4, fig. 1). Drooping wires are seen in plate 4, figure 2, and plate 5, figure 1, ready for the harvesting of the hops, while plate 5, figure 2, shows the wires pulled upward to their original position after the hops and cords have been removed. The hops are gathered in baskets, which are emptied into huge canvas containers, and the pay of each worker is according to the quantity of hops that he or she gathers. It was interesting to see the more active pickers help the older or less capable workers by emptying an occasional basket of hops into their containers.

The Indians employed in the hop fields are from widely separated localities, as stated, and many faces show the mixture of races which is common in British Columbia. This appears in the woman and her child from Kamloops (pl. 6, fig. 1) and in the portraits of singers and informants.

By a fortunate circumstance, two young men in the hop-picking camp had been at Neah Bay, and were acquainted with the writer's work. They were cousins, F. Knightum and Wilson Williams by name, and lived at Carmanah, 5 miles from Nitinat Lake. They had taken their fish across the Strait of Juan de Fuca to sell at Neah Bay, and had often heard the Indians tell of recording songs. Other Nitinat besides themselves attended the celebration of Makah Day, at which the writer was present. As a result of this acquaintance, the Nitinat were ready to consider the work favorably and consented to record 35 songs, many being the songs used in the treatment of the sick, which are usually difficult to obtain. Their influence assisted in the securing of songs from other groups in the camp.

Twenty-one singers were employed, the total number of recorded songs being 121. These singers came from 16 localities. The songs recorded and not transcribed were studied; many were found to resemble the transcribed songs so closely as to be without value, while others were not of sufficient interest to be transcribed.

Interesting data on the hunting of sea lions were obtained from Francis James, who lives on Cooper Island. These facts are not connected with any song, but form part of the general information concerning Indians of western British Columbia.

Francis James said that his people hunt sea lions, starting on the hunt about the last of March. Sometimes they are able to get sea lions on the eastern side of the channel, almost at the mouth of the Fraser River. It was customary, in old days, for 14 canoes to go on such a hunt,. and spears were used in killing the animals, but the most important members of the expedition were the men who knew the words that would make a sea lion stop. There were only one or two such men with an expedition and they learned the words from their old people. A sea lion might be going far away, but when a man spoke these words it would turn back and get in such a position that it could be speared. The words were *spoken*, not *sung*.

Sometimes a sea lion was captured that weighed a ton, and sometimes the sea lion was so strong that it upset a canoe, or dragged the canoe a long way, but when the sea lion "began to die" all the men threw their spears into it. Sometimes the wounded animal lived all night, and an effort was made to get it to go toward the shore, the canoes, by their ropes, trying to drag it in that direction. The ropes had "floaters" attached to them, similar to those on the whale-ropes of the Makah.

When the sea-lion hunters arrived at home, the meat was divided and there was a great feast. The man who first threw the spear into the sea lion received only the fin. The man who threw the second spear received the most meat and helped to divide it among the others. The hind quarters were considered the best portion of the meat, but the fin was the finest delicacy. It was customary to smoke the meat and keep the fat to eat with dried salmon. The hide was formerly used for the making of gun cases.

TREATMENT OF THE SICK

Two men who are engaged in treating the sick at the present time consented to record a portion of the songs which they use and to describe their methods. These men were Tasalt (pl. 6, fig. 2), who lives near Chilliwack, B. C., and John Butcher, who lives at Lytton, on the Thompson River. Both are men past middle age, but in sturdy health, working in the hop fields and living in the camp while hop picking is in progress.

Tasalt is commonly known as Catholic Tommy. The name Tasalt is inherited from a remote past and he does not know its meaning. In manner and mode of life he is quiet. H. Harding, Chief of Municipal Police in Chilliwack, has a wide and intimate acquaintance with Indians throughout the region, but did not know that Tasalt treated the sick, until the present material was obtained. Although living in the hop-pickers' camp, Tasalt was not in one of the communal houses. Instead, he lived in a shack located in the rear of a building on the edge of the camp (pl. 7, fig. 1). It seemed scarcely a habitation for a human being, even as a temporary abode, but it had the advantage of privacy. Tasalt's wife is a cripple, lying on a rough wooden bunk while he is absent at work. The roof is low and little light enters the place, yet in these surroundings the writer found this interesting medicine man.

Songs are the chief means employed by Tasalt in treating the sick. His mother was a doctor, but did not teach him and gave him no songs. He has received all his songs from spirits. His wife sings and drums while he treats the patient. He does not draw his hands along the patient's body, which is a method used by John Butcher (cf. p. 24), but he "gets the sickness and throws it away." After this has been done, he tells the patient not to eat much, and the sick man rests and sleeps. In a severe case he must work two or three times, but after the "sickness has been taken out" the person regains his strength rapidly. No material remedies are used. All sorts of cases are brought to him and he treats them all, having special songs for certain illnesses. He said that he had been able to help all except two of these cases, but "when he sees the sick person gradually disappear so that only the clothes remain, he gives up." He allows the persons in the room to cry if they wish to do so. This is forbidden in many tribes because of a belief that it will reduce the power of the doctor who is treating the sick person. In these tribes, the relatives of the patient and all who are in the room are asked to sing with the doctor in order to augment his power by their own. Tasalt requires no assistance except that of his wife.

When the purpose of the present work had been explained to Tasalt, he said that he would record his songs for the treatment of smallpox, fever, palsy, hemorrhage from the lungs, and pneumonia. Five songs were recorded, and it was supposed the entire series had been obtained, so the subject of inquiry was changed. About a week later, Tasalt returned, and said that he did not record the song for the treatment of pneumonia and wished to record it in order to fulfill his promise. He explained that the first song he recorded was in the nature of an introduction and should not have been counted as part of the series. He came again and recorded his song for the treatment of pneumonia, following it with his own dancing song (not transcribed), after which he said that he had finished his contribution of songs. The sources of the songs for the treatment of smallpox, fever, and pneumonia were not designated, but the other two were received 'from spirits not hitherto mentioned in connection with the treatment of the sick.

The introductory song and the songs for the treatment of smallpox and fever are similar in character (Nos. 1, 2, and 3). They are soothing melodies, framed by the descending tetrachord B flat–A–G–F and the tetratone (incomplete tetrachord) G–F–D. The opening measures are practically the same in these songs. The phrase indicated as the rhythmic unit is not repeated with accuracy, as in other songs, but contains interesting variations. The occurrences of this phrase are indicated by consecutive letters in the three songs (A to O), the only duplications occurring in the phrases G and I, and the phrases E and N. In these, as in other songs used by Indian doctors, it appears that the basis of musical therapy among the Indians consists in the use of subtle rhythms, and in variations of rhythm that hold the attention of a listener.

After singing each song as transcribed, Tasalt repeated a portion of the melody, taking care to bring his performance within the length of the phonograph cylinder. Each song has its own characteristic quality and the partial rendition of one song could not be mistaken for that of another. The first song contains 33 ascending, and 40 descending intervals. Approximately the same number of ascending and descending intervals occurs in the two songs next following, showing that the length, as well as the form, of the song was clear in the singer's mind.

No. 1. Introductory Song With Treatment of the Sick

(Catalog No. 2031)

Recorded by TASALT

Voice ♩ = 60
Drum ♩ = 60
See drum rhythm below

Drum rhythm

Free translation.—This person is going to cure me and I will be very glad when I am cured.

Analysis.— The characteristic of this song is its positive quality, expressed chiefly by an equal emphasis on the first and second counts of the measures in the rhythmic units (cf. No. 42). Attention is directed to this count in phrases A, C, and E, the first note on this count being a repetition of the preceding tone. The alternate phrases (B and D) are distinctly cheerful, with a bright, crisp division of the second count. The ascent from F to G, which has occurred frequently throughout the song, is changed to the ascending series G–A–B flat in the fourth from the final measure. Other drum rhythms are shown with Nos. 11, 14, 27, 28, and 59.

No. 2. Song When Treating Smallpox

(Catalog No. 2032)

Recorded by TASALT

Free translation.—I am curing you. I am going to take you and cure you.

Analysis.—The chief characteristic of this melody is the succession of minor thirds at the close of each phrase. The division of the first count of the rhythmic unit is alternately two sixteenth notes followed by an eighth and the reverse.

In the practice of Tasalt, a person suffering from fever was not allowed to drink water.

No. 3. Song When Treating Fever

Recorded by TASALT

(Catalog No. 2035)

Free translation.—Strengthen me, make me live, dear spirit.

Analysis.—The opening of this song is more direct than the two preceding, which it so closely resembles in many respects. The first tone is accented, not preceded by a short, unaccented tone as in the preceding songs. The melody moves more freely, and descends to the final tone by several descending intervals. It is interesting to note the downward glissando and the short pause in the opening portion of the melody.

A spirit called ha'wil gave the next song to Tasalt. This spirit was said to live in the water and to resemble a dog, but it had a golden breast and golden eyes. The song was used for severe cases of shaking palsy.

No. 4. Song When Treating Palsy

(Catalog No. 2036)

Recorded by TASALT

Free translation.—I am hawil and I am going to take the disease away.

Analysis.—The rhythm of this song is particularly steady and well defined, which would adapt it to its purpose. No rhythmic unit occurs and the song contains frequent changes of measure lengths but the steady quality is maintained. Alternate measures end with a rest except in the closing measures. Attention is directed to a melodic phrase which occurs on the first count of the fifth and ninth measures. A swaying of the melody in successive descent and ascent is restful and soothing and was noted also in the songs of a Yuma doctor (cf. Densmore, 1932, Nos. 40, 41, 42, and 43).

Tasalt said that he learned the next song when he was "training to be a doctor," and that he received it from a "wild spirit" called skeup'. He could not describe this spirit but said the spirits went away when the white men came.

No. 5. Song When Treating Hemorrhage From the Lungs

(Catalog No. 2033)

Recorded by Tasalt

Free translation.—I am going to cure this hemorrhage (the last word being an imperfect pronunciation of the English word).

Analysis.—The structure of this is different from the other healing songs recorded by Tasalt. There is no rhythmic phrase and the melody flows smoothly within its compass of ten tones. The downward and upward swaying of the melody, mentioned in the song next preceding, appears also in this song, with its soothing effect, while a certain liveliness is introduced by means of the divided triplets of eighth notes in the fourth and fifth measures. The ear expects the same at the opening of the sixth measure, but the first tone is prolonged and is followed by several triplets. This is the gentlest melody recorded by Tasalt, with no rhythms that would excite a patient.

No. 6. Song When Treating Pneumonia

(Catalog No. 2034)

Recorded by Tasalt

Analysis.—In this song with its short, almost jerky rhythm, we find a contrast to the preceding songs of this group. The time is broken by rests and there is one rhythmic unit. The song has a compass of an octave, and the pitch of the lowest tone is four tones lower than in the preceding songs recorded by Tasalt. The slight break in the time caused by the 5–8 measure is interesting and was distinctly given. The tones occurring in the melody are B flat, C, E flat, F, and G, with B flat as the implied keynote. These constitute the first 5-toned scale (cf.

footnote, p. 71) in which the third and seventh above the keynote do not occur. This scale occurs rarely in Indian music under the present system of analysis, appearing only 21 times in 1,553 songs. Other occurrences in this series are Nos. 37, 43, and 94.

The second native doctor who recorded songs is John Butcher who, as already stated, lives at Lytton on the Thompson River. His native name is Skwealke, briefly translated "Dawn." He is not tall, but heavy in stature, with a bushy, iron-gray beard. John Butcher and his family live in "E" (pl. 2, fig. 1), one of the large, communal houses provided for the hop-pickers, and his cubicle is first at the right of the entrance. He is very industrious, working in the hop-fields all day, so it was necessary to record his songs in the evening, in the Red Cross shack (pl. 2, fig. 2). His granddaughter acted as his interpreter.

Fasting is practiced by Butcher as a means of maintaining his power. It is said that he goes into the mountains and sometimes remains 7 or more days without food. During this time he sees the "little people," who are like Indians, but about 3 feet in height. They run around with sickness between their hands and put it into the people. Butcher gets it out, throws it away, and tells the little people to go away. While he is in the mountains, he talks with the animals who are his helpers, and they show him medicinal plants, telling their uses. (Cf. p. 29; also Densmore, 1922, pp. 127–128.)

When treating illnesses of a general character, Butcher puts his hands in water and then lays his hands on the sick person's head and moves them downward to his feet, then he "seems to hold the sickness in his two hands," and he makes motions as though throwing it away somewhat as though he were throwing a ball. In his treatment he sings, and then goes away, returning the next day. It is usually necessary for him to visit a sick person three times. No one sings with him unless the patient is very sick. In such a case he gets another doctor to help him and both sing.

The healing songs he recorded are those he uses in a case of confinement and are the first songs of this class that have been recorded by the writer. (A song for this purpose was recorded among the Seminole in Florida in 1933.) If a birth is delayed, he puts his hands in water and "rubs the patient's abdomen." Aside from this, his treatment of such cases is entirely by means of songs. He said the deer is a particularly good helper in such cases and that by its aid the child comes quickly and with little pain to the mother.

The first song of the series mentions two girls on a horse, the first girl telling the one who sits behind her to strike the horse to make it go faster.

No. 7. Two Girls on a Horse

(Catalog No. 2048, *a* and *b*)

Recorded by JOHN BUTCHER

Introduction

Song

Free translation
Poor sister, hit the horse,
Good-bye, my friend.

Analysis.—The introduction to this song contains only the tones A and B flat. The phrases are generally two or four measures in length, each followed by a rest of at least a quarter note duration. In its repeated semitones the melody conveys an impression of stark suffering, yet it is a gentle melody, seeming to express also the sympathy of the doctor.

The healing songs used by John Butcher are characterized by a sixteenth note followed by a rest, occurring in the opening measures of this song and on the accented count of the rythmic unit. The melody tones are F, G, A, and B flat, with G as the implied keynote. In tone material and in prolonged tones, this melody resembles a portion of the Makah and Clayoquot songs recorded at Neah Bay, Washington. The progressions are small, 17 of the 40 intervals being whole tones. The measures transcribed in 5–8 time were uniformly sung in all the renditions, and the long rests were uniform in duration.

In the next song, the doctor talks to a sturgeon and to a bird. The words of the interpreter are retained in the translation. It is interesting to note that the doctor does not ask that his own powers be strengthened, but that aid be extended to the patient. The same concept is expressed in the Chippewa tribe by the words translated "take pity," the phrase being frequently used to denote the attitude of supernatural beings toward members of the human race.

No. 8. "Look at This Sick Person"

(Catalog No. 2049)

Recorded by JOHN BUTCHER

Free translation
Go easy on this sick person,
Look at this sick person and go easy.

Analysis.—The most prominent tone in this song is B, and the melody progresses chiefly between B and A sharp, with single occurrences of G sharp and C sharp. After singing the song as transcribed, the singer began at the opening measures, but did not give an accurate repetition, occasionally varying the length of unimportant tones or substituting two sixteenth notes for one eighth note.

The free use of rhythm by this singer is shown by the slight differences in the rhythmic units of this and the two songs next following, these units being shown separately for convenience in comparison (p. 29). Only one duplication occurs, the second unit in No. 9 being like the fourth unit in No. 10. In two instances a phrase designated as a rhythmic unit in one song occurs once in another song. The length of the tones was clearly defined throughout these songs, and the slight differences in the phrases show a remarkable preception of rhythm on the part of the singer.

Two songs were taught to Butcher by his father whose name meant Road. The melody was the same in the two songs and the transcription is from the first song. In this the doctor talks to the seal, grizzly bear, and deer, and in the second song he talks to the eagle. Before recording these songs Butcher spoke a few sentences which were translated as follows: "I hope the sick person gets well. It will be awful if she goes away and dies."

No. 9. An Appeal to Certain Animals

(Catalog No. 2050)

Recorded by JOHN BUTCHER

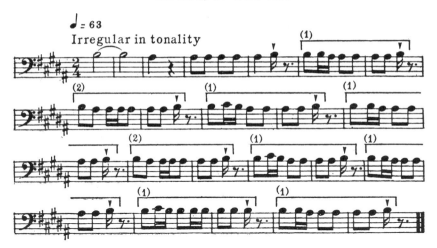

Analysis.—The phonograph record of this song is about two minutes in duration, with no repetition of the sequence of phrases here presented. The transcription is terminated arbitrarily, as in some of the healing songs of the Yuma. A large portion of the intervals are approximately semitones. The small compass, noted in songs recorded at Neah Bay, consists of a fundamental tone and the adjacent tones above and below. The time was maintained with great regularity.

The recording of the next song was ended abruptly. A group of men had gathered around the door of the shack where the songs were being recorded, and Butcher said they would be harmed by hearing these songs. In the portion recorded, he calls upon the deer, and there is a pause during which he imitated the sounds made by a deer. This was said to mean that the deer heard and answered his appeal. He said that if he had continued he would have called upon the grizzly bear.

No. 10. An Appeal to the Deer

(Catalog No. 2051)

Recorded by JOHN BUTCHER

Pause, with imitation of voice of a deer

Analysis.—An examination of this melody shows a prominence of a minor third in the portion before the voice of the deer is supposed to be heard, and a prominence of a whole tone thereafter. Three-fourths of the intervals are whole tones. This and the two songs next preceding are on the same pitch and in approximately the same tempo, showing the ability of the singer to hold both pitch and tempo.

John Butcher said that the songs for success in hunting had the same melodies as the songs for treatment of the sick, but appealed to the animals for success in hunting. A song of this sort, recorded but not transcribed, did not duplicate the melody of any recorded song for the sick, but was in the same style, with the same prolonged tones. Butcher sings this before going to hunt, so he will have good luck. The words are:

Going out to hunt deer, going to get my gun, and I scared up a big bear. I killed a deer and let the bear eat it.

Reference has already been made to the following comparison of rhythmic units in songs recorded by this singer.

Rhythmic Units in No. 8

Rhythmic Units in No. 9

Rhythmic Units in No. 10

Information concerning the treatment of the sick by Nitinat medicine men was obtained from two cousins, F. Knightum and Wilson Williams, who came from Carmanah, a village on Vancouver Island. They were accustomed to sing with their grandfather while he treated the sick, and in this manner they learned his songs. Their grandfather's name was Y'ak, a Nitinat name which has no known meaning. The Nitinat medicine men were said to confine their activities to helping the sick, "not throwing sickness at other people, as is done in some other tribes."

The Nitinat use herbal remedies for minor ailments and injuries. Some major illnesses and conditions are treated by "sucking out the difficulty" and others by passing the hands downward over the patient's body and then "throwing away the sickness," in a manner already described. Knightum said that if a man were injured and "the blood settled," his grandfather would suck out the trouble; he also "sucks out little worms, kills them, and throws them away." He does not give any herbal remedies.

Four sources of their grandfather's power were described by the informants, these being the wolves, the whales, the spirits of the dead, and the thunderbird. The first will be mentioned in connection with the treatment of the sick. Knightum said that his grandfather once speared a whale which talked to him, and therefore a whale helps him at the present time. The spirits of the dead sometimes come to him and give him songs to use in treating the sick. (Cf. Densmore, 1929 a, pp. 115–135.)

Y'ak treats a sickness which has been put into human beings by "little people who live in the mountains and come down"; he also treats sickness caused by other human beings, his method being the same for both. In this treatment, the patient lies on his back and Y'ak, using native red paint, makes a drawing of a wolf on the man's chest. He then takes a piece of soft cedar bark, puts it on the sick man's head, and begins to sing. During the treatment, he puts his hands on the picture of the wolf, draws them down to the man's feet and "throws the sickness away" by casting it from his fingertips. The treatment is always given at night and he allows the people to cry if they are moved to do so.

The songs of this medicine man are in groups of four and he calls upon one or another of his sources of power as he feels that the case requires. He usually sings 3 or 4 nights with a sick person, this time being sufficient for a cure, and sings different songs each night, changing them as he likes. Among the Nitinat, as in some other tribes, the number of singers is increased if the patient is very ill, thus enabling more persons to add their power to that of the doctor. Knightum said that if a person is very sick his grandfather "needs lots of singers" and that "everybody sings." The songs are accompanied by beating on an ordinary hand drum. While singing these songs, his grandfather "sees everything, all over the world." The words of these songs are summarized in the titles, and, with one exception, contain the affirmation which characterizes the songs of Indian doctors.

No. 11. "I Am Going to Cure This Sick Man"

(Catalog No. 1691)

Recorded by F. KNIGHTUM

Voice ♩ = 108
Drum ♩ = 108
See drum rhythm below

Drum rhythm   *Fine*

Analysis.—The first four tones in this melody are the principal tones occurring in the song. They constitute a minor triad and minor seventh, a group of tones found in particularly primitive melodies. The occurrence of G as a passing tone completes the material of the second 5-toned scale. It is a forceful melody, containing no change of measure lengths and progressing by 10 ascending and 11 descending intervals. Other occurrences of the 5-toned scale are Nos. 15, 18, and 65 (cf. footnote, p. 71).

No. 12. "I Am Trying to Cure This Sick Man"

(Catalog No. 1693)

Recorded by F. KNIGHTUM

Voice $\boldsymbol{\mathsf{J}}$ = 100
Drum $\boldsymbol{\mathsf{J}}$ = 100
Drum rhythm similar to No. 11

Free translation.—I am trying to cure this sick man as I treated when I first began to be a doctor.

Analysis.—This is a melody of unusual simplicity, containing only the tones of the major triad. In its emphasis on the first count of the measures and in its general effect of firmness, it resembles a majority of the other songs attributed to Y'ak. This personal peculiarity in a man's songs is seldom noted in Indian music and suggests that Y'ak was a man of strong character. The song contains 9 ascending and 10 descending progressions.

An interesting attempt at part singing occurred during the recording of this song, another singer "putting in extra tones" softly, during prolonged tones of the melody (cf. p. 48).

No. 13. "The Whale Is Going to Help Me Cure This Sick Man"

(Catalog No. 1694)

Recorded by F. KNIGHTUM

Voice ♩ = 96
Drum ♩ = 96
Drum rhythm similar to No. 11

Analysis.—This melody is framed chiefly on four descending tetratones (incomplete tetrachords), these being C–B flat–G, B flat–G–F, G–F–D, and F–D–C, followed by a descent from D to G. The song closes on C and is transcribed as having F for its keynote, though its tonality is not established. It resembles the song next preceding in the use of a half note on the first count of the rhythmic unit.

No. 14. "The Thunderbird Will Help Me Cure This Sick Man"

(Catalog No. 1692)

Recorded by F. KNIGHTUM

Voice ♩ = 100
Drum ♩ = 108
See drum rhythm below

Drum rhythm
♩ ♩ ♩ ♩ ♩ ♩

Analysis.—Five sorts of intervals occur in this song. To this variety is due, in part, the cheerful and lively character of the melody. Attention is directed to the discrepancy in the metric unit of voice and drum, each tempo being steadily maintained.

The three songs next following were recorded by Y'ak's grandsons, but no information was obtained concerning their use.

No. 15. Song of Y'ak, the Medicine Man (a)

(Catalog No. 1695)

Recorded by F. KNIGHTUM

Voice ♩ = 104
Drum ♩ = 104
Drum rhythm similar to No. 11

Analysis.—A decided contrast is noted between this and the four preceding songs attributed to the same man. This song is more lively, contains shorter note value, and has two rhythmic units. The tone material is the same as that which formed the framework of No. 11, but this song contains no passing tone. The song contains no change of measure lengths, and the ascending and descending intervals are equal in number. Attention is directed to the occurrence of a triplet of eighth notes on an accented count in the first, and an unaccented count in the second rhythmic unit.

No. 16. Song of Y'ak, the Medicine Man (b)

(Catalog No. 1715)

Recorded by WILSON WILLIAMS

Voice ♩ = 112
Drum ♩ = 112
Drum rhythm similar to No. 11

Fine

Free translation.—I hope you will be cured by me.

Analysis.—The rest which occurs in the rhythmic unit of this song is always preceded by an ascending and followed by a descending interval. Rests in the rhythmic unit of an Indian song are somewhat unusual. This song contains three double occurrences of the rhythmic unit, with connective measures in different rhythms, giving variety to the rhythm of the song as a whole. The last 10 measures were omitted in some renditions, the connective measure being introduced at this point and the singer returning to the opening of the melody. With the exception of three intervals, the song progresses by minor thirds and whole tones.

No. 17. Song of Y'ak, the Medicine Man (c)

(Catalog No. 1716)

Recorded by Wilson Williams

Voice ♩ = 112
Drum ♩ = 112
Drum rhythm similar to No. 11

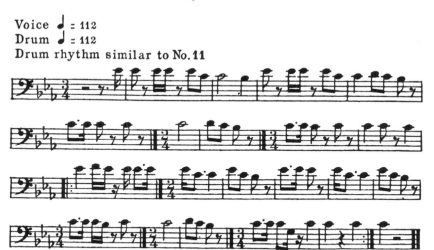

Analysis.—A peculiarity of this song is the short tones followed by short rests. Several renditions were recorded, this exclamatory style being carefully maintained. The rhythm is more interesting than the progressions, which consist chiefly of minor thirds and whole tones. Drum and voice were synchronous throughout the performance.

Another song used by Y'ak, the medicine man, was studied but not transcribed, as it contained no peculiarities that have not already been noted in his songs.

The next singer said his father was a doctor and received songs from a spirit which appeared to him in the mountains. It was his father's custom to go into the mountains and remain without food. Once he became ill, after remaining without food or water for 2 days, and a spirit came and helped him, so that he did not die. The spirit looked like a woman and changed its appearance, so that sometimes it was large and sometimes small. This spirit became his constant helper. He saw it whenever he went into the mountains and it gave him songs. The interpreter, about 32 years old, said this man was his uncle and that, as a child, he saw the man going away to the mountains. No description of his treatment of the sick was obtained. This is one of his songs:

No. 18. "This Song Cheers Me"

(Catalog No. 2026)

Recorded by JIMMIE O'HAMMON

Voice ♩ = 56
Drum ♩ = 76
Drum rhythm similar to No. 11

Free translation
For a long time I have been walking and seeing nothing;
Now I find this song and it cheers me.

Analysis.—This melody is based on the interval of a fourth, which is often associated with motion in men, birds, or animals. This interval occurs first between B and E, then as A descending to E, while the song closes with E descending to B in the lower octave. The two latter intervals contain a passing tone. The tone material is that of the second 5-toned scale. Attention is directed to the difference in tempo of the voice and drum, this difference being steadily maintained.

Annie Tom recorded a song used by her grandfather, who was a doctor and obtained his power from the thunderbird. The words form the title and contain the affirmation which characterizes many Indian songs used in treating the sick.

No. 19. "I am Going to Make You Better"

(Catalog No. 1711)

Recorded by ANNIE TOM

Voice ♩ = 52
Drum ♩ = 52
Drum rhythm similar to No. 1

Fine

Analysis.—This peculiar song was sung once, after which the repeated portion was sung four times. The intonation on the tone transcribed as D sharp in the opening measures was somewhat uncertain, approaching E if the phonograph were freshly wound, thus increasing its speed and slightly raising the pitch. The chief interest of the song lies in its rhythm, which was maintained throughout the performance. The beat of the drum is rapid, consisting of four beats to one time unit of the melody.

Bob George said that his grandfather was a doctor and that the next was his personal song. The singer heard his father sing it and learned it in that manner. His father died in 1920 at the age of about 100 years. This indicates the age of the song.

No. 20. Doctor's Song (a)

(Catalog No. 1667)

Recorded by Bob George

Analysis.—An alternation of double and triple measures characterizes this song, the first of each measure being strongly accented except in the third and seventh measures. The first phrase contains four and the second phrase contains five measures, the additional length being secured by a change of accent on a quarter note in the latter portion of the phrase. It is a cheerful, pleasing melody and yet, to our ears, it has a plaintive character. This may be due to the prominence of the subdominant in the eight measures preceding the close.

No information was obtained concerning the next two songs except that they belonged to doctors.

No. 21. Doctor's Song (b)

(Catalog No. 1668)

Recorded by BOB GEORGE

Analysis.—Only three tones occur in this song, but the variety in the movement and rhythm produces an agreeable melody. The song contains 32 measures and 54 progressions, all of which are whole tones. Attention is directed to the prominence of E, the tone above the keynote, and to a comparison between the last two occurrences of the rhythmic unit.

No. 22. Doctor's Song (c)

(Catalog No. 1669)

Recorded by BOB GEORGE

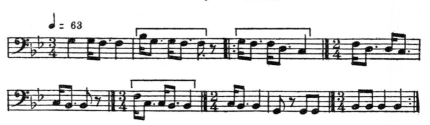

Analysis.—In this melody we have an interesting example of thematic treatment, the triple measures in the opening portion being followed by two double measures that extend the rhythmic unit. A minor third comprises about one-fourth of the intervals. The keynote is regarded as B flat, the melody being classified as on the fourth 5-toned scale. Other songs based on this scale are Nos. 31, 79, 85, 91, 92, and 95. (Cf. footnote, p. 71.)

No. 23. Song of a Medicine Man at Nitinat Lake (a)

(Catalog No. 1696)

Recorded by F. KNIGHTUM

Voice ♩ = 88
Drum ♩ = 88
Drum rhythm similar to No. 11

Analysis.—Three renditions of this song were recorded, the transcription being from the second. Attention is directed to the portion of the song beginning with the seventh measure. There was little accent in this portion and the division into measures is somewhat arbitrary, but the time value of the eighth note was maintained. This is a semirecitative and in other renditions we find the same general melodic pattern, but not an exact duplication of phrases. The principal interval is a descending whole tone which comprises 20 of the 50 progressions. This and the descending minor third, which occurs frequently, were sung somewhat glissando, producing a soothing effect.

No. 24. Song of a Medicine Man at Nitinat Lake (b)

(Catalog No. 1697)

Recorded by F. KNIGHTUM

Voice ♩ = 72
Drum ♩ = 72
Drum rhythm similar to No. 1

Analysis.—The transcription of this song is from the first rendition, the remainder of the performance containing the characteristic phrases, but no exact repetitions. Attention is directed to the fourth measure from the close with its explosive accent on the second count. The slow tempo and small intervals occurring in the open measures of the song suggest gentleness, while the short, crisp phrases followed by short rests are full of energy, intensified by the rapid beats of the drum. More than three-fourths of the intervals are whole tones, occurring chiefly in descending progression.

It is the custom in many tribes to designate a man only by a nickname. The doctor to whom the next song belonged was known as "Doctor Jim." He had been dead for many years, but was remembered as a "good doctor."

No. 25. Doctor Jim's Song

(Catalog No. 1719)

Recorded by KATHERINE CHARLIE

Voice ♩ = 63
Drum ♩ = 63
Drum rhythm similar to No. 11

Fine

Analysis.—Drum and voice were synchronous in all the renditions of this song, the drumbeats being distinctly given. The first portion of the melody is based on the descending and ascending interval of a fourth, and the second portion, with a different rhythm, is based upon consecutive whole tones. With one exception the progressions are whole tones and minor thirds.

A certain medicine man living at Carmanah is able to locate lost persons and articles. It is his custom to dance with his arms held out and shaking, his fingers extended and trembling, this manner probably being in accordance with his dream. It was said that a man once went out hunting and became lost. This doctor danced for about 3 hours before he was able to locate the man, then he told the people where they would find the hunter. The people went to the place indicated by the doctor and there they found the man. His song has no words.

No. 26. Song of a Medicine Man at Carmanah

(Catalog No. 1698)

Recorded by F. KNIGHTUM

Voice ♩ = 80
Drum ♩ = 84
Drum rhythm similar to No. 11

Analysis.—In this agitated melody with its slight changes in repetition we find a contrast to the calm, reassuring songs of Y'ak, a contrast which corresponds to the methods employed by the two men. Eight renditions of this song were recorded, the first phrase showing three variations, as indicated in the three renditions which are presented. The drum is slightly faster than the voice, each tempo being maintained through the performance.

WAR SONGS

The customs of war differ among the tribes represented at Chilliwack, and songs from three localities were recorded. The largest group is from the Nitinat, who cut off the heads of their enemies, a custom which also prevailed among the Makah (Densmore, 1939, pp. 184–185). These songs are very old and have come down from the time when the Nitinat used spears and knives in war. The following song was sung when they were ready to embark in their canoes for a war expedition.

No. 27. Song When Going to War

(Catalog No. 1699)

Recorded by F. KNIGHTUM

Drum rhythm: Quarter notes in opening measures followed by

Analysis.—This melody begins on the first of the measure and is characterized by force and directness. The drumbeat was variable and consisted of quarter notes, changing to eighth notes accented in groups of two, with an occasional return to the quarter-note beat. The fourth is prominent in the framework of the melody and, as in other songs having this characteristic, the keynote is not fully established. The song is, however, considered minor in tonality. Five renditions were recorded without a break in the time.

Occasionally the Nitinat went on foot to seek the enemy, the following song being sung by warriors returning on foot. The Nitinat have no horses at the present time, depending upon their boats for transportation.

No. 28. Song When Returning From War

(Catalog No. 1700)

Recorded by F. KNIGHTUM

Voice ♩ = 96
Drum ♩ = 96
See drum rhythm below

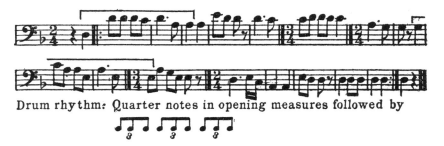

Drum rhythm: Quarter notes in opening measures followed by

Analysis.—Three descending fourths are prominent in the framework of this melody. The melodic trend resembles that of the song next preceding and, as in that song, D is regarded as the keynote.

The opening ascent of an octave was noted also in several Chippewa war songs. Six renditions of this song were recorded and show unimportant differences which occur more frequently in melodic progressions than in the rhythm. The singer took breath in various places, after the manner of young singers, the indicated rests being given in the rendition which was selected for transcription. The drumbeat was in quarter notes during the earlier rendition,* changing to the triplet rhythm in the third rendition, but showing occasional beats in quarter-note time.

In the dance that followed a war expedition, each warrior held his spear diagonally across the front of his body and, as he danced, he thrust the point of the spear upward above his left shoulder, this constituting a gesture of the dance.

---

*In music above, for "opening measures," read, "first renditions."—F. D.

No. 29. War Dance Song

(Catalog No. 1701)

Recorded by F. KNIGHTUM

Voice ♪= 168
Drum as indicated

Analysis.—Five renditions of this peculiar song were recorded, the transcription being from the third. This is the first song recorded by the writer in which the drumbeat is so slow that it cannot be measured by the metronome. The interval between drumbeats varies slightly, as indicated, and it appears from a comparison of the renditions that the player was guided by the relation between drum and voice rather than by an effort for a steady rhythm in the drum. The melodic differences in the other renditions consist chiefly in the addition of passing or ornamental tones and in the omission of an occasional phrase. An example of ornamentation in other renditions is the substitution of two sixteenth notes (C–B flat) for the second eighth note (B flat) in the second measure. The song has a compass of 11 tones and omits the fourth tone of the octave. The ascending and descending intervals are almost equal in number, the latter comprising five each of fourths, major thirds, minor thirds, and whole tones, with one semitone. Such uniformity in progressions is unusual in the songs under analysis.

The heads of the enemy were carried on poles in the dances that followed a victory. The two songs next following were sung in such dances and were accompanied by drums and by the striking together of sticks. These songs are still sung by the Nitinat in their dances.

No. 30. Song When Carrying Heads of the Enemy on Poles (a)

(Catalog No. 1702)

Recorded by F. KNIGHTUM

Voice ♪ = 184
Drum as indicated

Analysis.—This song is characterized by a slow drumbeat similar to that in the song next preceding. Four renditions were recorded and show no differences except in the drumbeat, which varies slightly. The transcription is from the first rendition. The song contains 27 progressions, 17 of which are whole tones.

No. 31. Song When Carrying Heads of the Enemy on Poles (b)

(Catalog No. 1703)

Recorded by F. KNIGHTUM

Analysis.—Several renditions of this song were recorded, the one selected for transcription being that in which the metric unit is nearest to a quarter-note. It is a wild, barbaric melody, sung with much freedom. This song contains short, explosive tones like those which occurred in preceding war songs, but does not have the slow drumbeat which characterized the preceding songs. It is based on the fourth 5-toned scale and progresses chiefly by whole tones.

From the Sliamon and Homalko Reserve comes the song of a dance that was held when captives had been ransomed and brought home. The ransom was paid in blankets. This song was sung at such a dance, the men carrying a knife in one hand and a gun in the other.

No. 32. Song Concerning a Ransomed Captive

(Catalog No. 1672)

Recorded by BOB GEORGE

Analysis.—The two ascending progressions at the opening of this song are aggressive, and are followed by an unbroken descent of six tones. Five renditions were recorded, followed by a short pause, after which the singer began upon C sharp instead of C natural, continuing his performance on that pitch level.

Tasalt, whose songs in treating the sick have been presented (Nos. 1–5), said that his tribe were not head hunters and had been at war during his lifetime, using bows, arrows, and spears. He recorded two very old songs used in war dances. These songs are connected with a tradition of a man who rode on a mythical creature of the deep, called kohaks. It is said that a dangerous water spirit lived in the Strait of Juan de Fuca and the man rode upon the kohaks far out on the water, killed the bad spirit, and returned, making a safe landing. By this he protected his people from danger and was qualified to become a warrior.

No. 33. The Rider on the Kohaks

(Catalog No. 2039)

Recorded by TASALT

Free translation.—I am riding out on the kohaks.

Analysis.—The principal tones in this melody are B flat and C. The song is based on a major triad and sixth, but the form is unusual, the keynote occurring only on the last half of an unaccented count. The rhythm is somewhat jerky and difficult to show in notation. About two-thirds of the progressions are minor thirds and whole tones.

The savage spirit of ancient warfare is shown in the words of an old song recorded by Anna George who lives at Sardis. This war song belonged to her great-grandfather whose name was George, and she intends to teach it to her children, requesting them, in turn, to teach it to their descendants so that it may be preserved. The words of the song are "Don't you scream. I am a woman and I am going to hit you." The song was not transcribed.

POTLATCH SONGS

The man who recorded the next song is from the town of Hope, on the Fraser River. At a potlatch his people used two sorts of rattles. The man who gave the potlatch used a rattle consisting of a container enclosing small pebbles or shot, while the leaders of the ceremony used rattles made of shells. A rattle made of pecten shells on a hoop of whalebone was used by a Makah doctor (Densmore, 1939, pl. 14, *d*).

The next song is that of the guests arriving at a potlatch and dancing as they come from their canoes. The host does not go to meet them, but remains to welcome them at his door. A similar performance was witnessed at Neah Bay, when the guests at the Makah Day celebration danced up the shore from a large canoe in which they were supposed to have arrived from distant homes. Some had small drums and the motions of the dance were individual. The approach to the place of the celebration was remarkably picturesque. A portion of the dances at this celebration was shown in the writer's paper on Nootka and Quileute Music (Densmore, 1939, pls. 22, 23, 34).

Men and women joined in this song, which was said to be particularly fine when sung "in parts." The addition of harmonic parts to a native melody has been seldom noted among the Indians. It may be an evidence of musical influence from the white race.

No. 34. Song of Approach to a Potlatch

(Catalog No. 2046)

Recorded by DENNIS PETERS

Voice ♩ = 72
Drum ♩ = 76
Drum rhythm similar to No. 11

Analysis.—The ease with which "parts" could be added to this song is shown by its tone material. The melody contains the tones of the major triad, with the sixth occurring three times. The compass of six tones lies entirely above the keynote, the largest interval being a major third. Ascending and descending intervals are about equal in number.

No. 35. A Desire for Clear Weather

(Catalog No. 2037)

Recorded by TASALT

♩ = 50

Free translation.—It will be nice for all the people if the weather clears.

Analysis.—The tempo of this song is unusually slow and the manner of singing the prolonged tones is characteristic of the songs of this region. The division of the first count is effective and occurs twice in the song. There is an unusual number of rests, which were given clearly in all the renditions.

The next song was inherited in the family of the singer and was sung by the host before distributing the presents at a potlach. The prolonged, high tone at the opening of the song may have been intended to attract the attention of the guests.

No. 36. Potlatch Song

Recorded by ANNIE TOM

(Catalog No. 1710)

Voice ♩ = 72
Drum ♩ = 132
Drum rhythm similar to No. 14

Analysis.—Four rhythmic periods form the length of this song, the rhythm of the first differing from the others in its opening measure. The intervals consist of three whole tones, occurring chiefly in descending progression. While E is suggested as a keynote, the tonality of the melody is not established. The first note of each measure, especially in the upper register, was sung with a decided accent. Five renditions were recorded and show no differences.

The following explanation of a potlatch was given by Francis James, who lives on Cooper Island. James said that when he was a little boy it was the custom for a man to give a potlatch in order to collect the debts owing to him. If his friends had borrowed money and it was time for payment, he announced that he would give a potlatch, and told those who owed him money that he expected them to attend. They came and returned the money. When he had received payment for all the debts, he gave presents to the people who had returned the money, perhaps a blanket or similar gift, and sometimes he gave them money. (Cf. Densmore 1939, pp. 72–95.)

A song of the host at a potlatch was recorded by Dennis Peters, but was not transcribed as similar songs have already been presented. He said the host at a potlatch entered with a blanket wrapped around him, singing a song inherited in his family. The singers joined in this song. The host danced during the song and then gave away his blanket. The song was repeated with the gift of each valuable article. Between the repetitions of the song and during the bestowing of the gifts there were sounds which can only be described as prolonged howls. An old person might give such a howl while the host was singing. The host would then stop singing and give the person the blanket or other gift which he had in his hand, after which he would take up another article and resume his song.

DANCE SONGS

Dennis Peters, who recorded the next three songs, is a particularly intelligent Indian, living at Hope. He said that, at a season of the year which he thought to be December, the old-time Indians living on the Fraser River were seized with a malady resembling fits, and they "had to dance to get over it." The affliction returned every year and lasted about a month. There were special songs for this dance and the songs used by the men were different from those used by the women. He said that his own people discontinued this custom 20 or 30 years ago, but that it is still kept up by people living on the lower Fraser River Sometimes the people fainted and remained unconscious (or semiconscious) for 2 hours, during which time they wept aloud. "A whole lot of singers had to get around them and sing before they could get up." The emotional excitement suggests a connection between this and the cult of Smoholla, or Skilmaha, also that of the Shakers, whose meetings were held regularly at Neah Bay, when the Makah songs were recorded.

The dances at this annual event were of two sorts, the first being a slow dance with a rapid drum and the second being a dance with a great deal of motion and jumping. While the drum was said to be faster than the voice in the opening songs of this dance, the difference is in the number of beats in the first song, the drum being in eighth-note values while the song contains longer tones. In the second song of the group, the drum has a much faster metric unit than the voice, with shorter note values.

It appears this dance had power to benefit the sick, as Peters related the following incident which was known to him: A young man's brother was seriously burned with gasoline, and the young man felt himself responsible for the accident. He lost his voice, and the Indian doctors were unable to help him. Finally, they said he would regain his voice only when dancing. Accordingly, a dance was given for his benefit, and the moment he began to dance he regained his voice. He has, however, been "sickly" ever since the event. It is interesting to note this coincidence of the use of gasoline and a primitive belief in healing.

This and the song next following are those of the slow dance with rapid drum.

No. 37. Dance Song of the Fraser River Indians (a)

(Catalog No. 2040)

Recorded by DENNIS PETERS

Voice ♩ = 76
Drum ♩ = 76
Drum rhythm similar to No. 11

Analysis.—Two interesting phases of this song are its tone material and its thematic structure. The tone material is that of the first 5-toned scale, in which the third and seventh tones above the keynote do not occur.[2] The rhythmic unit is simple and occurs twice in the opening phrases. The seventh and eighth measures show two characteristic count divisions separated by a quarter note, and the tenth measure shows the rhythmic unit changed by an even division of the first count. These contrasts give interest to the rhythm of the song as a whole. The melody contains no change of measure lengths and has a compass of 9 tones.

The next song is for the same part of the dance but belongs to a different village.

No. 38. Dance Song of the Fraser River Indians (b)

(Catalog No. 2041)

Recorded by DENNIS PETERS

Voice ♩ = 92
Drum ♩ = 144
Drum rhythm similar to No. 11

Analysis.—Attention is directed to the discrepancy between the metric unit of voice and drum in this performance. The prolonged tones of the song are also

---

[2] Other songs on this scale are Nos. 6, 43, and 94. Cf. footnote 3, p. 71.

unusual. A group of two eighth notes occurs on both the accented and unaccented counts of the measure. The melody contains all the tones of the octave, which is unusual in the songs of British Columbian Indians.

The next song is that of the rapid dancing in which the people jumped from the ground, and in which the "dancing was *even* with the drum." The change of motion occurs "after they have been around two or three times."

No. 39. Dance Song of the Fraser River Indians (c)

(Catalog No. 2042)

Recorded by DENNIS PETERS

Voice ♩ = 84
Drum ♩ = 84
Drum rhythm similar to No. 11

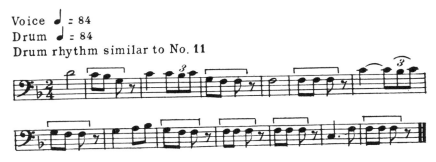

Analysis.—This is a more fluent melody than the two songs immediately preceding. It opens with an interesting phrase and closes with an ascending interval of a fourth. More than half the progressions are whole tones.

The next song affords an example of two interesting customs, the insertion of new words in an old song and the use of mispronounced English words. The tune was said to be very old and the words "Klismus payah" are inserted between native words, occurring in the eighth measure. The song was sung at Christmas and the words are readily identified as "Christmas presents." The frequent high tones have a suggestion of eagerness. These are followed by descending series of tones. Annie Tom is from the Nitinat village on Vancouver Island.

No. 40. Dance Song (a)

(Catalog No. 1704)

Recorded by ANNIE TOM

Voice ♩ = 108
Drum ♩ = 108
Drum rhythm similar to No. 14

Analysis.—Seven renditions of this song were recorded, the only difference being a slight variation in the note values of the opening measures. The consecutive eighth notes are effective in contrast to the other rhythms, and the sixteenth rest near the close of the song was clearly given in all the renditions, terminating a neat, short phrase.

The next song was sung when "going toward a partner" in the dance.

No. 41. Dance Song (b)

(Catalog No. 1705)

Recorded by ANNIE TOM

Voice ♩ = 96
Drum ♩ = 132
Drum rhythm similar to No. 14

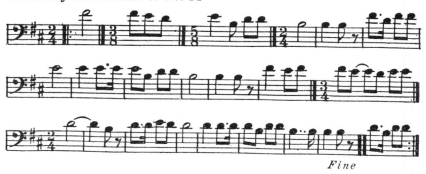

Fine

Analysis.—The duration of the three opening measures in this song is equivalent to three measures in double time, but the melody is transcribed according to the accents given by the singer. The tempo changes slightly during the song, but the tempo of the drum does not correspond to either tempo of the voice. Twenty-three of the 27 intervals are minor thirds and whole tones.

The two songs next following have no words and are used in social dances.

No. 42. Dance Song (c)

Catalog No. 2047)

Recorded by DENNIS PETERS

Voice ♩ = 66
Drum ♩ = 66
Drum rhythm similar to No. 14

Analysis.—A peculiarity of this melody is the equal stress on the first and second counts of the measures, though the song is felt to be in double rhythm (cf. No. 1). A second peculiarity is the descending sequence of two whole tones ending on the keynote. These tones are rapid, as in Nos. 65 and 70. All the phrases begin with an ascending progression. The rhythmic unit occurs in the first and last portion of the melody, the middle portion showing a slight, but interesting difference in rhythm. The fourth is a prominent interval in the melody, two ascending fourths constituting an ascent of a seventh, midway through the song.

The next song was said to be very old.

No. 43. Dance Song (d)

(Catalog No. 2024)

Recorded by JIMMIE O'HAMMON

Voice ♩ = 66
Drum ♩ = 66
Drum rhythm similar to No. 1

Analysis.—This is an interesting example of a melody on the first 5-toned scale in which the third and seventh above the keynote do not occur. The sixth above the keynote is a prominent interval and suggests a major tonality. The song has a compass of nine tones, lying partly above and partly below the keynote. The melody shows unusual variety in form though it contains only three intervals other than minor thirds and whole tones.

The following song of the Klokali was said to be very old. The Klokali is an important ceremony of tribes on the northwest coast and was formerly held in midwinter, continuing 6 days and closing with dramatic dances on the beach. The modern Klokali is solely for pleasure and lasts only 1 day. According to Swan (1870, pp. 66, 67),

The ceremony of the great Dukwally, or the Thunder bird, originated with the Hesh-kwi-et Indians, a band of Nittinats living near Barclay Sound, Vancouver Island.

Swan then relates the legend of the young man who was dragged on the stones of the beach, saying the chief of the wolves was so pleased with the bravery of the young man that he imparted to him all the mysteries of the Thunderbird performance. A song connected with this legend appears as No. 74, p. 78. A description of the Klokali among the Makah and Clayoquot is contained in Nootka and Quileute Music (Densmore, 1939, pp. 101–128).

No. 44. Klokali Dance Song

(Catalog No. 1706)

Recorded by ANNIE TOM

Voice ♩ = 88
Drum ♩ = 88
Drum rhythm similar to No. 14

Analysis.—The phonograph cylinder contains nine renditions of this melody, after which the singer gave the opening interval, prolonging the high tone to more than twice its transcribed length and allowing the voice to slide downward in a howl. The Klokali songs recorded at Neah Bay, as well as the songs when towing a dead whale, were terminated in this manner. Triple and double measures alternate in this song, each measure beginning with a marked accent. The song contains seven measures and only seven progressions.

The Nitinat Indian who recorded the next song said the Thunderbird dance is danced every year, in the latter part of July, by his people. The costume consists of a blanket with eagle feathers suspended along the edge, the dancer extending his arms as he dances. The gift mentioned in the song may be "about one dollar."

No. 45. Thunderbird Dance Song

(Catalog No. 1717)

Recorded by Wilson Williams

Voice ♩ = 80
Drum ♩ = 144
Drum rhythm similar to No. 14

Free translation.—I am going to give my money to the other people.

Analysis.—A peculiarity of this song is the discrepancy between the tempo of voice and drum, each being steadily maintained. The metric unit of the drum is not a multiple of that of the voice. Five renditions were recorded and show no differences except the omission, in two renditions, of the eighth and ninth measures. This number of renditions is valuable for comparison as the song is unusually difficult. The tones are those of the minor triad and fourth and the song contains no change of measure lengths.

No information was obtained concerning the next song except that it was connected with the "Campbell dance," in which wooden head-dresses were worn.

No. 46. Song of Campbell Dance

(Catalog No. 1673)

Recorded by Bob George

Voice ♩ = 88

Analysis.—This is similar to many songs heard among tribes of the north woodland region. It progresses entirely by minor thirds and whole tones except for the ascending fourth at the opening. No unit of rhythm occurs, the entire song having a rhythmic unity which cannot be divided into phrases. There is no change of measure length, and the several renditions are uniform in every respect.

No. 47. Dance Song From Babine

(Catalog No. 1690)

Recorded by ABRAHAM WILLIAMS

Voice ♩ = 104

Analysis.—As this is the only song obtained from Indians living at Babine it is interesting to find it a melody with so much individuality. An ascent of a tenth in three measures is very unusual in Indian songs, yet it occurs twice in this melody, each time with a return to the original tone. Three other phrases ascend a fourth and return to the original tone. Thus the tone D, which is the lowest tone of its compass, occurs at the beginning and end of five phrases. The song contains all the tones of the octave except the second and sixth and, except for two ascending octaves, it progresses entirely by minor thirds and whole tones.

The songs of a certain social dance of the Thompson River Indians were accompanied by a drum and by the striking together of two sticks, the latter accompaniment being similar to that heard at Neah Bay. It has also been heard among the Menominee of Wisconsin and the Choctaw in Mississippi. Men and women took part in this dance.

No. 48. Dance Song of the Thompson River Indians (a)

(Catalog No. 2055)

Recorded by HENRY McCARTHY

Voice ♩ = 76
Drum ♩ = 76
Drum rhythm similar to No. 11

Free translation.—Everybody, come and dance.

Analysis.—This melody moves freely within its compass of eight tones. Slight differences occurred in the four renditions and, as an example of such differences, the second rendition is presented as well as the first. The principal interval is a minor third.

No. 49. Dance Song of the Thompson River Indians (b)

(Catalog No. 2056)

Recorded by HENRY McCARTHY

Voice ♩ = 69
Drum ♩ = 96
Drum rhythm similar to No. 11

Free translation.—Sing, everybody sing.

Analysis.—The melodic structure of this song is based upon two whole tones with a larger connecting interval. Attention is directed to the discrepancy between the tempo of voice and drum.

The three songs next following were those of a dance in which a wooden headdress representing a wolf was worn. The circumstances under which the songs were recorded made it impossible to secure information concerning the dance.

No. 50. Song of Dance With Wolf Headdress (a)

(Catalog No. 1712)

Recorded by ANNIE TOM

Voice ♩ = 100
Drum ♩ = 132
Drum rhythm similar to No. 14

Analysis.—The compass of this song is lower than that of white women's voices, a peculiarity noted in a majority of songs recorded by Indian women. The song consists chiefly of repetitions of a rhythmic unit except the phrase beginning with C in the third measure. This change in rhythm gives character to the melody.

No. 51. Song of Dance With Wolf Headdress (b)

(Catalog No. 1713)

Recorded by ANNIE TOM

Voice ♩ = 120
Drum ♩ = 120
Drum rhythm similar to No. 11

Analysis.—A sharp, crisp manner of singing, as well as an emphasis on the first tone of each measure, characterizes this song. Six sorts of ascending intervals occur, which is an unusual variety of these progressions. It is interesting to note the difference between the measures which follow the rhythmic unit in its three occurrences. In the first instance, a 2–4 measure leads the melody upward while, in the second and third instances, a 3–4 measure ends the phrase abruptly on a low tone. The third occurrence of the rhythmic unit is followed by a succession of measures in quarter and eighth notes, without the dotted eighths which occurred in the preceding portions of the song.

The next song was sung when the dancing began.

No. 52. Song of Dance With Wolf Headdress (c)

(Catalog No. 1718)

Recorded by KATHARINE CHARLIE

Voice ♩ = 108
Drum ♩ = 132
Drum rhythm similar to No. 14

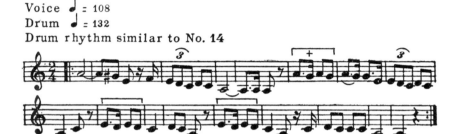

Analysis.—Five renditions of this song were recorded and in all of them the singer gave a clear intonation on G sharp in the second measure; the next occurrence was slightly lower, and the third was sung as G natural. This suggests that the pitch of the first tone was above the natural range of the singer's voice. The discrepancy between the tempo of voice and drum was steadily maintained. The song contains 17 measures and 40 progressions, which is an unusual freedom of movement.

SOCIAL SONGS

It is customary for a person to sing and dance alone after receiving a gift. This was seen at Neah Bay, on the celebration of Makah Day, in 1926. The recipient of a gift sang and "danced," standing still and turning the body from side to side while the hands were upraised with palms forward, on a level with the elbows. This resembled the positions in Makah honor songs (Densmore, 1939, pl. 21, *a, b.*)

Gifts are presented to visitors near the close of a gathering, which explains the words of the next song.

No. 53. Song After Receiving a Gift (a)

(Catalog No. 1707)

Recorded by ANNIE TOM

Voice ♩ = 92
Drum ♩ = 144
Drum rhythm, similar to No. 14

Free translation.—Good-bye my friend, I am going away.

Analysis.—An interesting discrepancy between the tempo of voice and drum occurs in this song, and was steadily maintained during the five renditions. The chief interest of the melody lies in the frequent use of the fourth, and in the measure that was sung between the renditions. The singing continued after the end of the phonograph cylinder had been reached but, from listening to the singing, it appears that the end of the melody is on E, as indicated in the transcription.

It is probable that the person who sang the next song had received a gift of money at a dance. He was impressed by the amount and thought he might afford a room at the village hotel, which is regarded as the height of luxury.

No. 54. Song After Receiving a Gift (b)

(Catalog No. 1708)

Recorded by ANNIE TOM

Voice ♩ = 100
Drum ♩ = 152
Drum rhythm similar to No. 14

Free translation.—How much money for a room in the hotel?

Analysis.—Several points of unusual interest occur in this melody. The metronome indication of voice and drum is as accurate as possible by the scale of the instrument, and it will be noted that, within the duration of a measure, the voice has two metric units and the drum has three units. Voice and drum were synchronous on the first count of each measure, and the time of each was steadily maintained. Attention is next directed to the similarity between the first phrase of the song and the connective phrase, in which the words occur. The latter is the more melodious and differs in the position of the rest. The rhythmic unit is preceded and followed by various rhythms. Except for one ascending fourth, the only intervals are minor thirds and whole tones. The song has the unusual compass of 11 tones, both the highest and lowest tones being distinctly sung.

There was no dancing with the next four songs, and it was said that "everybody sang." The man who recorded the songs lives on Powell River.

No. 55. Social Song (a)

(Catalog No. 1674)

Recorded by Bob George

Analysis.—Except for two larger intervals, this melody progresses entirely by minor thirds and whole tones. The measure lengths change frequently and the trend of the song is steadily downward. Attention is directed to the third occurrence of the rhythmic unit in which the third count is divided differently than in the first occurrence, giving variety to the rhythm, yet continuing the principal accents. The song contains all the tones of the octave except the fifth and is melodic in structure.

No. 56. Social Song (b)

(Catalog No. 1675)

Recorded by Bob George

Analysis.—Several renditions of this song were recorded and show no differences. The melody is characterized by a variety of ascending intervals, four sorts of upward progressions occurring, while the descending intervals consist of minor thirds and whole tones. It is a pleasing melody, major in tonality and containing all the tones of the octave except the seventh.

The next two songs are very old, the singer having learned them from his father.

No. 57. Social Song (c)

(Catalog No. 1676)

Recorded by BOB GEORGE

♩ = 58

Fine

Analysis.—Attention is directed to the count divisions in the second measure of this song, which occur with a different accent in the fifth and sixth measures. The song has no rhythmic unit and it appears there is no rest in the melody as the singer introduced an eighth rest at a different point in each rendition, the pause being apparently for taking breath. Many bytones were introduced but cannot be shown in notation.

No. 58. Social Song (d)

(Catalog No. 1677)

Recorded by BOB GEORGE

♩ = 69

Analysis.—This song is classified in the key of D major although the keynote occurs only in the second and fifth measures from the close. The tone C sharp is the most prominent tone in the opening measures and is the highest tone of the compass. The latter portion of the song is characterized by an unbroken descent in each phrase. The melody has a compass of 10 tones and contains all the tones of the octave except the fourth.

SLAHAL GAME SONGS

The playing of the slahal game is common to many tribes in the Northwest. The game among the Thompson River Indians is described by James Teit, who states that it is known to the whites as "lehal." This authority states further, that—

Many Spences Bridge women used to play it, and had a different song for it from that of the men. Lower Thompson women seldom or never played this game. [Teit, 1900, p. 275.]

The implements of the slahal game are two bones, differently marked, and the action consists in hiding the bones in a player's hands, the opponents guessing their position. In a small game only one pair of bones is used, but at Chilliwack, in the game witnessed by the writer, two pairs of bones were used, each being hidden by one man. These bones are highly valued by their owners, but one man consented to lend a pair to be photographed (pl. 7, fig. 2).

Age and long use have yellowed and polished these bones, which were made from a bone of the hind leg of an ox, the ends tipped with brass. One bone is decorated with a band midway its length and was called the male, while the other, with decorations near the end, was called the female.

The game is played outdoors and the number of players is according to the available space, an average number being 34. The players are divided into two "sides," and kneel on the ground in two lines, facing each other. A heavy plank is in front of each line of players, slightly elevated above the ground to give resonance as they pound upon it with short sticks. When two sets of bones are to be used, a man in the middle of each line acts as leader of his side and designates a man toward his right and another toward his left to hide the bones while the opponents guess their location. After a certain score has been made, the playing changes sides and those who were guessing take their turn at hiding the bones. On being requested by the leader, each man takes a pair of bones and puts his hands under a coat that lies across his knees while he arranges the bones to his satisfaction, concealing one in each hand. The two men then raise their hands in the air and move them rhythmically to and fro with many gestures, according to individual fancy. Their companions sing and a majority pound on the plank but, in the game at Chilliwack, two or three at the end of the line pounded on drums (pl. 8). In these games the guessing was done by the opposing leaders, seated in the middle of the line, others guessing only by his permission. It was said that the expression of the face, which, in some games, may betray the location of a hidden article, did not form a factor in slahal, but that the guessing "depends on the good judgment of the guesser." According to this informant, the relative location of the bones "will go all one way for a while," and skill depends largely on a study of averages and probabilities, making success a matter of study rather than skill.

The guesses are indicated by signals given with the thumb and forefinger of the right hand, each signal indicating the location of both bones in the hands of both players. Only four combinations are possible, these being (1) with the unbanded bones in the hands nearest each other, (2) with the unbanded bones in the hands farthest apart, (3) with the unbanded bones toward the guesser's left hand, and (4) toward his right. If the guesser decides upon the first combination, he points toward the ground; for the second combination, he indicates his guess by a spread of thumb and forefinger; and for the third and fourth, he points to the hand of either player which, in his opinion, contains the bone without a band. Figure 2 shows three of the possible combinations.

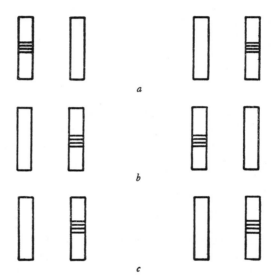

FIGURE 2.—Sketch showing locations of bones in slahal game.

A slahal game was played every Sunday afternoon at Chilliwack, extending far into the evening, a huge bonfire giving sufficient light. Occasionally the game was played in the evening during the week. The firelight on the rows of swaying, singing men was picturesque, and, during a portion of the period, the moon was full, shining on the snow on the mountain tops and the square lines of the camp buildings, making a background for the scene. A hundred or more men and women stood behind the players or were grouped in the vicinity.

The games at Chilliwack were for pleasure, though there was some betting. Their purpose was "to make the old people happy," and men who were known to be poor players were allowed to hide the bones if they wished to do so. Good feeling prevailed, as people from widely separated localities joined the game, which they were accustomed to play at home.

The traditional origin of the slahal game was related by Jimmie O'Hammon, chief of a band of Squamish Indians living on the Squamish River. He is known as "Chief Jimmie Jimmie" and his group is known as O'Hammon's Band (cf. p. 86). He said that slahal was played before the flood, when all the people spoke the same language. Only one bone was used at that time and the players "hugged themselves with their arms" when playing. After the flood, there still were people who played the game, but many languages were spoken and the people were "all split up." When Christ came and changed the people into animals, there were some who were not changed, and they preserved the game, so it has come down to the present day. An old song "about Christ changing some of the people into animals" was recorded, but not transcribed.

The following song is very old and is concerning a man who dreamed about the slahal bones. The words of the song were said to be about his dream, but they have been forgotten. The dream may have been concerning the origin of the game, or it may have been a dream in which a man was told how he might become a successful player. In the latter case, the song would be sung by his companions when he was hiding the bones. (Cf. Densmore, 1913, pp. 210, 212.) The phonograph record contains the "squeals" of the women as in the next song.

No. 59. Slahal Game Song (a)

(Catalog No. 2028)

Recorded by JIMMIE O'HAMMON

Voice ♩ = 84
Drum ♩ = 84
See drum rhythm below

Drum rhythm

Analysis.—A peculiarity of this song is the meter of the drum, three even beats of which are equal to one count of the melody. This occurs in no other song recorded at Chilliwack. The rhythm of voice and drum were steadily maintained in all the renditions. The melodic progressions are all major seconds except the two minor thirds at the close of the song. In rhythmic structure, the song consists of five periods, each containing two measures. The ascent to the closing tone carries the melody forward to its repetitions.

Concerning the next song, the singer said it was used "before Christ changed some of the people into animals." He said his stepfather sang it to him when he was a child. There are sounds on the phonograph record that were said to be "the squeals of the women when a score stick was thrown." It is not unusual for Indians to record the sounds that are incident to the singing of a song, when they record the melody.

No. 60. Slahal Game Song (b)

(Catalog No. 2023)

Recorded by Jimmie O'Hammon

Voice ♩ = 126
Drum ♩ = 126
Drum rhythm similar to No. 11

Analysis.—Only a portion of this performance is transcribed, the remainder consisting of similar phrases. In this somewhat monotonous melody there is a distinct rhythmic unit. The second measure of this unit is slightly varied in its repetitions. Each measure began with a strongly accented tone; this exclamatory manner of singing gambling songs has been noted in several other tribes. (Cf. Densmore, 1922, Songs Nos. 96 and 98.)

No. 61. Slahal Game Song (c)

(Catalog No. 2052)

Recorded by Otter Billie

Voice ♩ = 56
Drum ♩ = 56
Drum rhythm similar to No. 1

Analysis.—This song is characterized by a slow tempo and rapid drum. The singer's voice is low in range and the song begins and ends on the keynote, which is the lowest tone of its compass. The ascending and descending intervals are the same in both number and size, each group consisting of two minor thirds and three major seconds. No change of measure length occurs in the melody, this peculiarity, together with the prominence of the keynote, giving a steadiness to the song which would assist its use with the game.

No. 62. Slahal Game Song (d)

(Catalog No. 2053)

Recorded by Otter Billie

Voice ♩ = 56
Drum ♩ = 56
Drum rhythm similar to No. 1

Analysis.—While the tempo and rhythmic unit in this are the same as in the song next preceding, the characteristics of the melody are entirely different. This song is major instead of minor in tonality, has a much larger compass than the preceding, and contains lyric passages. The measure in triple time near the close of the song is particularly vigorous and, with the preceding tone, represents an ascent of an octave within three counts. In some renditions, a sixteenth note on E takes the place of the first rest in the third and seventh measures, giving the melody a smoothly flowing quality.

No. 63. Slahal Game Song (e)

(Catalog No. 2054)

Recorded by OTTER BILLIE

Voice ♩ = 96
Drum ♩ = 96
Drum rhythm similar to No. 11

Free translation.—When I took the bones, I beat.

Analysis.—The chief peculiarity of this song is the two-measure phrase which ends on an accented tone and is followed by a short rest. Such phrases constitute the entire melody. The ascending and descending intervals are equal in number and size, each comprising 5 minor thirds and 20 whole tones. The jerky, emphatic rhythm is characteristic of songs which were heard during the playing of this game. The words refer to the game implements, which, as stated, are short bones, concealed in the player's hands.

No. 64. Slahal Game Song (f)

(Catalog No. 2057)

Recorded by HENRY McCARTHY

Analysis.—This song is peculiar in that the third above the keynote occurs only as the highest tone, this occurrence being in the third measure. The most prominent tone is E, the tone above the keynote, this being the accented tone in 7 of the 10 measures. The fourth is a prominent interval, 2 descending fourths carrying the melody downward in the third and fourth measures. The rhythm is more broken than in the preceding slahal game songs, with more frequent rests and no decided accents.

The singer of the next song is from the Sliamon Reserve on Powell River.

No. 65. Slahal Game Song (g)

(Catalog No. 1671)

Recorded by BOB GEORGE

Analysis.—This interesting melody contains the tones of the second (minor) 5-toned scale.[3] The intonation was excellent, and drum and voice coincided throughout the performance. Like many other songs recorded from this locality, the melody moves freely, having a large number of progressions and being lyric in character. This may be due to the influence of the Roman Catholic Church with its tuneful melodies, although missions of this Church have been present in tribes which did not have these fluent melodies. It is interesting to note that the songs here presented are the first songs recorded by Indians who live beside large rivers.

The next song was sung after a slahal game, but could be sung at any time.

---

[3] The 5-toned scales considered in these analyses are the five pentatonic scales according to Helmholtz (1885, p. 269), described by him as follows:

"1. *The First Scale,* without Third or Seventh (sequence of tones G, A, C, D, E).

"2. *The Second Scale,* without Second or Sixth (sequence of tones A, C, D, E, G).

"3. *The Third Scale,* without Third and Sixth (sequence of tones D, E, G, A, C).

"4. *The Fourth Scale,* without Fourth or Seventh (sequence of tones C, D, E, G, A).

"5. *The Fifth Scale,* without Second and Fifth (sequences of tones E, G, A, C, D)."

See also Densmore, 1918, p. 7.

No. 66. Song of Pleasure

(Catalog No. 2038)

Recorded by TASALT

Analysis.—The melodic plan of this song is simple. It begins on the octave, ends on the keynote, and gives prominence to the third and fifth above the keynote. It is, however, classified as melodic with harmonic framework because of the accented F in the third measure. A dotted eighth followed by a sixteenth note is a frequent count division but the song contains no phrase which can be designated as a rhythmic unit. The descending fourth is a particularly prominent interval and gives liveliness to the melody. The tone material is the fourth (major) 5-toned scale and the trend of the melody is steadily downward.

GAMBLING SONGS

Two gambling songs composed by Indians living on the Thompson River were recorded, though the game with which they were used was not designated. The singer of the next song lives at Boothroyd, a town on the Fraser River, and recorded only this song and one other (p. 94).

No. 67. Gambling Song (a)

(Catalog No. 2058)

Recorded by ANNIE BOLEM

Fine

Analysis.—The uncertainty of intonation by this singer made the song difficult to transcribe until a delicate adjustment of the speed of the phonograph gave the present alinement of intervals. An effort was made to preserve the song because it is a valuable example of interrupted rhythm. The purpose of the song was to baffle and confuse the opponents, for which the rhythm is admirably adapted. The only tones are the keynote and its second, third, and fourth. Whole tones comprise 14 of the 18 progressions.

No. 68. Gambling Song (b)

(Catalog No. 2063)

Recorded by Julia Charlie

Analysis.—This melody progresses with unusual freedom and alternation of ascent and descent. The characteristic progression is a descending whole tone which comprises more than half the intervals. Rests occur frequently in the song, dividing it into short phrases, yet the rhythmic unit comprises five measures. The song contains no change of measure length. A slight change of rhythm occurs in the third period, a peculiarity frequently noted in Indian songs.

CANOE SONGS

Among the most characteristic songs recorded at Chilliwack are those that were sung when paddling the canoes. It was said that 10 or 15 persons often went in a canoe and that everyone sang. The words of the first song were said to be "Roman Catholic," and the songs were sung "when taking the priest from place to place."

In these charming songs we feel the rhythm of the canoe moving through deep but quiet waters. Around is the magnificence of the mountains and we seem to see the wonderful lights and shadows of the far north. The songs are happy and suggest safety. These Indians living on Powell River did not encounter the storms that beat upon the land of the Clayoquot, on the west coast of Vancouver Island. The river was a highway and they sang as they paddled their canoes from one village to another.

No. 69. Canoe Song (a)

(Catalog No. 1665)

Recorded by Bob George

Analysis.—The peculiar rhythmic effect of this song is partially due to the continuous double time, the character of the two rhythmic units, and the decided accents on the first of the measures in which the units do not occur. The units are alike except that in one the complete measure is preceded by a tone and in the other is followed by a tone, thus giving a swaying effect. The thirty-second rests were followed by an unaccented tone too short for transcription, on which the syllable *ki* was sung, the syllable *a* following on the accented tone. This melody is harmonic in structure and the tempo is slow. It was sung with a sustained tone and good intonation. Two renditions were recorded, each being once repeated.

No. 70. Canoe Song (b)

(Catalog No. 1666)

Recorded by Bob George

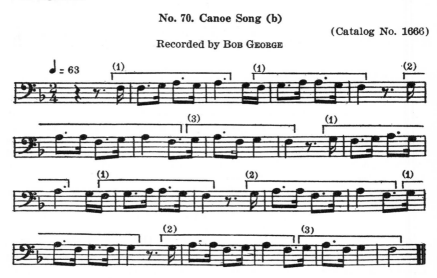

Analysis.—This, like the song next preceding, is without change of measure lengths. The only tones are F, G, and A, and the song swings back and forth within the compass of a major third, suggesting the motion of paddling a canoe. In rhythmic form, it is simpler than the preceding song and contains two rhythmic units, differing only on the final tones.

An Indian named Johnson, from Port Simpson, also recorded a canoe song. He said that each chief has his own canoe song and the people can tell who is coming by the song that is being sung. Ten or twelve men are in a canoe and they keep time to the song with their paddles. One man who knows the song is appointed to start it, and he repeats the words before they begin to sing. The man who steers the canoe gives the signal for the men to begin to paddle by saying, "Who-oo," with a prolonged tone.

No. 71. Canoe Song (c)

(Catalog No. 1682)

Recorded by Johnson

Free translation.—(*First rendition.*) There is rock where they are hammering a copper hiatsk. (*Second rendition.*) Nobody invited me. I am in a foggy place (confused and do not know where to go).

Analysis.—The structure of this melody resembles those recorded at Neah Bay and is different from other songs in this group and from songs of the Indians living at Powell River. It has a compass of four tones, comprising a keynote with the tone below and two tones above it. The tone E, regarded as the keynote, occurs in more than half the measures and is usually on an accented count. Ascending and descending intervals are about equal in number and the song contains only one interval (a minor third) that is larger than a whole tone.

STORIES AND THEIR SONGS

Henry Haldane (pl. 9, fig. 1), who related the first of these stories, lives at Port Simpson. He said that his grandfather's generation lived at Kitknont and his father's at Kitsala. He prefaced the story with the statement that thousands of years ago, when the flood came, his ancestors got into their canoe and drifted until the waters subsided; then they found themselves on Queen Charlotte's Islands. They camped near Skiddegate, on a place that now belongs to the Haida. They knew they were far from their former home, and so decided to stay there. They married the Haida and the party increased in numbers.

At one time a young boy of his father's people went trout fishing in a creek. They went up a creek and all fished. The boy was the chief's son. All the others in the party caught plenty of fish, but he could not get any, so he went down to the camp and cooked their trout. The boy sat down with the others and they gave him a trout on a plate. A frog jumped on the trout and the boy threw the frog away. As he was about to eat his trout, the frog jumped back again on his plate and, in anger, he threw the frog into the fire. He went to bed, and early next morning they started for home. While he was pulling hard at his oar, he heard a woman on the shore call, "Hey, take me in. I want to go with you." He looked and saw an old woman with a stick.

The boy said to his companions, "No, pull ahead." The old woman followed along the shore, but the boys would not take her in. Then she said, "See here, boys. When you get around that point, one of you will die in the canoe. So on, one after another will die until only one will get home. He will tell the tale and then die." It was said, "The old woman was a frog, and it was her daughter who came to the young man and wanted to marry him." [4]

When they passed the point indicated by the old woman, one of the young men died. This continued as the old woman had predicted, until only one reached home. He was the young man on whose plate the frog had jumped. He told the story and then dropped dead. The next day the people heard a woman coming down from the mountains. There was a lake behind the village. She sang and everybody went out to see her, and she cried. Then a fire came down from heaven and burned all those people. Mr. Haldane said, "That was why my father's people made this song for the children. When the old people were feeling good with liquor, my father took me on his lap and sang this kind of song for me."

No. 72. Song With Story of the Frog Woman

(Catalog No. 1681)

Recorded by HENRY HALDANE

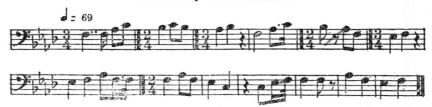

Free translation.—My brother killed a frog and thereafter the whole village burned to death. We came from the Haida. We all belong to the Haida, therefore my name is Chief Kala (name of singer's father).

Analysis.—This is a particularly fluent melody lying partly above and partly below the keynote. It is minor in tonality and progresses by minor thirds and major seconds, except for two major thirds and one fourth. The whole tone between the seventh and keynote is interesting, since many songs of minor tonality give little prominence to the seventh.

An old story was said to be "put into" the following song. A widow has gone crazy and she tries to sing. In the song she says, "I don't know where I am going. I am dressed up, but I take off my fine things and give them to poor orphan girls. You will see

---

[4] This sentence does not pertain to the story as related.

these girls dressed up. You must take a nice feather and wrap it around me because the fish took me thousands and thousands of years ago. I don't know where I am going." It is probable this is contained in the words of the song. The singer is from the Skeena River region.

No. 73. "Wrap a Feather Around Me"

(Catalogue No. 1686)

Recorded by JANE GREEN

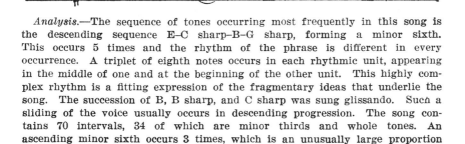

Analysis.—The sequence of tones occurring most frequently in this song is the descending sequence E–C sharp–B–G sharp, forming a minor sixth. This occurs 5 times and the rhythm of the phrase is different in every occurrence. A triplet of eighth notes occurs in each rhythmic unit, appearing in the middle of one and at the beginning of the other unit. This highly complex rhythm is a fitting expression of the fragmentary ideas that underlie the song. The succession of B, B sharp, and C sharp was sung glissando. Such a sliding of the voice usually occurs in descending progression. The song contains 70 intervals, 34 of which are minor thirds and whole tones. An ascending minor sixth occurs 3 times, which is an unusually large proportion of this interval.

The story of the man who dragged his body on the rocks in order to become a successful whaler was obtained among the Makah and holds an important place in the legends of the northwest coast (Densmore, 1939, p. 57). The singer, a member of the Nitinat tribe, said this was her father's song, and was sung by the Nitinat when towing a dead whale.

No. 74. "I Will Scrape My Body on the Rocks"

(Catalog No. 1709)

Recorded by ANNIE TOM

Free translation.—I will scrape my body on the rocks because I want to get a whale.

Analysis.—This peculiar melody lies chiefly within a compass of a minor third. It contains no rhythmic unit, but each phrase contains an ascending followed by a descending trend. The progressions are unusual and comprise 4 fourths, 2 minor thirds, 12 whole tones, and 10 semitones. The transcription is from the first rendition, the intonation on C natural being less clear in the later renditions.

The following story was told to little children: One day a chief was walking on the beach with his little boy. They saw a big whale which had been killed and was lying on the sand. The chief made a hole through the tail, and said, "Little boy, you had better jump through that hole." The song was sung in connection with the story, but the exact connection was not explained.

No. 75. The Little Boy and the Whale

(Catalog No. 2061)

Recorded by JAKE GEORGE

Voice ♩ = 88
Drum ♩ = 88
Drum rhythm similar to No. 14

Analysis.—This is a pleasing melody consisting of the tones F, G, and A, with one occurrence of B natural. The tone F is clearly the fundamental and the signature of the transcription is that of the key of F major. This signature is only for convenience of observation, the tone material being that of the key of C. In this instance the notation shows, in the simplest possible manner, the pitch and affiliation of the tones sung by the Indian, but does not carry the full significance in musical usage. Attention is directed to the ascending sequence of three whole tones, occurring about midway through the melody. Such a sequence is rare in recorded Indian songs. The progressions comprise 36 whole tones in ascending and the same number in descending order.

Among the Nitinat, as among the Makah and Clayoquot, the old women have a pleasant custom of going to a house and singing in honor of infants or little children, their songs being rewarded with food or gifts (Densmore, 1939, p. 215). Such songs usually represent the child as engaged in the actitivies of an adult, or praise its appearance.

No. 76. Song to a Little Girl

(Catalog No. 1714)

Recorded by ANNIE TOM

Voice ♩ = 88
Drum ♩ = 88
Drum rhythm similar to No. 14

Fine

Free translation.—Dear little girl, did you have a small face?

Analysis.—The framework of the first and second phrases in this song is a minor triad and minor seventh, and the trend of each phrase is upward, then downward. The principal interval is a whole tone. Five renditions were recorded, and in each rendition a descending glissando occurred near the close of the song, while the descending fourth, which constitutes the final interval, was sung without a glissando.

A song to put a child to sleep was recorded by a woman from Church House, on the Homalko Reserve. The words consisted of the admonition, "Go to sleep, go to sleep."

No. 77. Lullaby

(Catalog No. 1680)

Recorded by SOPHIE WILSON

♩ = 58

Analysis.—This melody consists of glissando phrases alternating with rapidly enunciated tones. It is impossible to indicate the progress of the glissando by ordinary notation, but the pitch of the highest and lowest tones were clearly sung. The tempo was maintained throughout several renditions.

LOVE SONGS

Dennis Peters, who lives on the Fraser River, recorded two songs of this class, both expressing the gentle loneliness which characterizes many Indian love songs. The first of the group was said to be the song of a woman who was separated from her husband and "made up a song about him."

No. 78. "I Wish I were a Cloud"

(Catalog No. 2044)

Recorded by DENNIS PETERS

Free translation.—I wish I were a cloud so I could stay always in the air and see my husband all the time.

Analysis.—A peculiarity of this song is the prominence of D, the tone above the keynote. An appealing quality is given by the ascending glissando in the first measure and by the five ascending fourths, while the drooping trend of the last seven measures suggests the depression implied in the words.

A different type of melody is presented in the next song, the words of which are summarized in the title.

No. 79. "All My Sweethearts Are Gone Except One"

(Catalog No. 2045)

Recorded by DENNIS PETERS

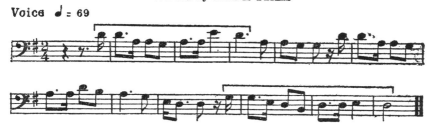

Analysis.—This pleasing melody has a compass of 11 tones, lying partly above and partly below the keynote. The tone material is that of the fourth 5-toned scale. The song consists of three periods, the first and third being designated as the rhythmic unit while the second differs slightly in rhythm. A resemblance to the song next preceding is seen in the frequency of ascending fourths and fifths.

A woman from the Skeena River country recorded the following song.

No. 80. "I Am Going to Stay at Home"

(Catalog No. 1687)

Recorded by JANE GREEN

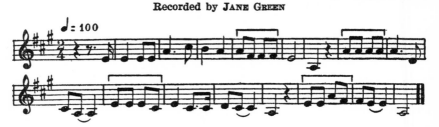

Free translation.—I was of two minds about going with you and now I have made up my mind to stay at home. I heard what you are doing, that is why I am going to stay at home.

Analysis.—This song is unusual in the number and variety of its progressions. The song contains 15 measures and 3 times descends an octave within 3 measures. Eleven sorts of intervals occur, 6 being in ascending and 5 in descending progression. The song is major in tonality and contains all the tones of the octave except the seventh. The rhythmic unit is simple and is preceded and followed by various rhythms which are not repeated. This is interesting in view of the words. The melody was not accurately repeated but the essential rhythms appear in all the renditions.

A love song recorded by Henry Haldane of Port Simpson was not transcribed. The rendition was preceded by the words, "I am going to sing a Haida love song," these words being recorded by the phonograph. The first verse was in the Indian language, and the words were translated, "O, my heart is broken because I did not see my girl, so I always cry." The second verse was in Chinook, and was translated, "Show me your kindness. Give me a drink and I will do the same for you in return." The singer said, "the Hudson's Bay people came among these Indians in 1862 and brought the Chinook." This suggests that the Chinook words may have been added to an older, native song.

The two songs next following are from the Nass River region.

No. 81. "She Is Glad to See Him"

(Catalog No. 1688)

Recorded by ELLEN STEVENS

Free translation.—She has been trying to see her sweetheart for a long time and is glad to see him.

Analysis.—Two renditions of this song were transcribed, the first rendition being here presented. The tone material is the same in the two renditions, but the first has the larger compass, using C in the upper as well as the lower octave. Successive renditions showed similar unimportant differences. Shrill cries were interpolated at the close of the ninth measure. The intervals are larger than in a majority of the British Columbian songs.

No. 82. "Give Me a Bottle of Rum"

(Catalog No. 1689)

Recorded by ELLEN STEVENS

Free translation.—When she got a sweetheart he offered her a drink and she said she wanted rum. If you want to give me a drink, give me a bottle of rum.

Analysis.—The fourth is a rather frequent interval in this melody, the other progressions being minor thirds and whole tones. The song is minor in tonality, harmonic in structure and contains all the tones of the octave. Two rhythmic units occur, separated by slightly different rhythms in their two occurrences. Beginning with the eighth measure from the close we find a phrase which suggests the first rhythmic unit.

DIVORCE SONGS

Two songs connected with an old custom of divorce were recorded by Jane Green from Skeena River. If a woman quarreled with her husband and was sent away, she gave a dance in about 3 days and her husband gave a similar dance 3 days after hers. Both spent much money on these dances and gave many presents. At the woman's dance about seven women stood in a row, about two arms' lengths apart, and moved their heads as they danced, while the woman who had been sent away by her husband stood still in the middle of the row. The people clapped their hands as they sang the following song. In explanation of the last portion of the words, it was said, "We have a story that if I travel and get lost somebody will touch me when I am almost dead and little mice will take me to a house and I will put some wool in the fire, and a little old woman will scrape lots of it under her blanket."

No. 83. Divorce Dance Song (a)

(Catalog No. 1684)

Recorded by JANE GREEN

Fine

Free translation.—In a little while. I guess you love me now. I guess you admire me now. You threw me away like something that tasted bad. You treat me as if I were a rotten fish. My old grandmother is going to take her own dry blackberries and put them under her blanket.

Analysis.—Certain resemblances occur between this and the song next following which is also a divorce song. Both songs begin in double time, have a compass of about an octave, and end on the keynote, which is the lowest tone of the compass. This song is in the key of B major, is based on the major triad and sixth, and contains only one interval larger than a minor third. The ascent to accented tones, occuring frequently in the first portion, gives a plaintive effect while the trend of the latter portion is steadily downward, the repeated tones at the close seeming to express a finality in the singer's mind.

The next song was also sung at a woman's divorce dance.

No. 84. Divorce Dance Song (b)

(Catalog No. 1685)

Recorded by JANE GREEN

Free translation.—I thought you were good at first. I thought you were like silver and I find you are lead. You see me high up. I walk through the sun. I am like the sunlight myself.

Analysis.—The change from major to minor tonality occurs in all the renditions of this song, the keynote remaining the same, but the third and sixth being lowered a semitone. The intervals are more varied than in the song next preceding and comprise two semitones and five intervals larger than a minor third. Without these intervals the melody would be monotonous, as the remaining intervals consist of minor thirds and whole tones, about equal in ascending and descending order. The first portion of the song is rather lively and is based on the interval of a fourth, but with the change to minor tonality the fourth is replaced by minor thirds. The final measures are slower in tempo and contain a rather sad but coherent phrase.

MISCELLANEOUS SONGS

The singer said she had heard the old people sing the following song. In explanation she said her people believe that the spirits of the dead make known their presence in a room by a slight explosive noise in the fire.[5] She said, "If you hear '*ping*' in the fire it is some dead person speaking. When he comes into the room he causes a thought of him to come into the minds of the people in the room, then he speaks through the fire." Continuing her narrative, she said that a spirit who does not want to speak through the fire makes known his presence in the woods by making a tree fall when there is no wind. "If a person is walking in the woods and sees a tree fall when there is no wind he will say 'Now you chopped down the big rotten tree.'"

[5] Cf. story of The Girl who Married the Fire Spirit (Swanton, 1909, pp. 239X240).

No. 85. Song to a Spirit in the Fire

(Catalog No. 1683)

Recorded by JANE GREEN

Free translation.—Who is dead that you feel so badly? I am very ashamed of you, still you are speaking after you are dead. You speak through the fire. I am not going to do that myself if I am dead. I am going to take an ax and chop down a tree.

Analysis.—This is a cheerful melody based on the fourth 5-toned scale. The fourth is a frequent interval, and the minor thirds and whole tones are equal in number. The song contains three phrases which are indicated as rhythmic units. A frequent change of measure lengths also gives variety to the rhythm.

The man who recorded the next song is chief of the O'Hammon Band of Indians living on the Squamish River. His name is the same as that of the band of Indians and was given as O'Hammon, O'Hammond, and O'Hammel, the first form being given on the best authority and used in the present paper. He is commonly called "Chief Jimmie Jimmie." The next song is concerning an Indian prophet named Skilmaha who lived in the vicinity of Hope about a century ago, "before the coming of the white man." This prophet foretold the coming of a different people and had many followers. It is probable that reference is made to Smoholla, the Dreamer of the Columbia River region, whose influence extended widely in Washington and Oregon and undoubtedly spread toward the north (Mooney, 1896, pt. 2, pp. 731–745). Smoholla was born in 1815 or 1820 (Mooney, 1896, pt. 2, p. 717) and the religion which he founded is described as "a system based on the primitive aboriginal mythology and usage, with an elaborate ritual which combined with the genuine Indian features much of what he had seen and remembered of Catholic ceremonial parade, with perhaps some additions from Mormon forms" (Mooney, 1896, pt. 2, p. 719).

No description of the teachings of Skilmaha was obtained, but it was said that he was subject to trances of a cataleptic nature. It appears that his power is challenged in the following song. The words show a knowledge of the Old Testament, contradicting the statement of the Indians that Skilmaha lived before the coming of the white man.

No. 86. Song Concerning the Prophet Skilmaha

(Catalog No. 2021)

Recorded by JIMMIE O'HAMMON

Free translation.—I would believe you if you would destroy us by fire.

Analysis.—The tone material of this melody is the key of E major and the song ends on the tone above the keynote (cf. Nos. 87 and 97). Its repetitions differ somewhat in note values, the song appearing to have more than one set of words, which affects the duration of tones. One half the progressions are whole tones.

The Indians of the Fraser River region terminate the period of mourning for the dead in a ceremonial manner. This custom was witnessed by the writer among the Chippewa and Menominee, and described among the Yuma and Cocopa Indians. (See Densmore, 1913, pp. 153–162; 1932, pp. 163, 164; 1932 a, pp. 73–85.) The following song was used at such a ceremony in British Columbia and belonged to the brother of a man who was drowned. It was called a "crying song."

No. 87. Song with Termination of Mourning

(Catalog No. 2027)

Recorded by JIMMIE O'HAMMON

Free translation.—I will cry as I walk and look up at the sky.

Analysis.—The tempo of this song is slow and it was sung with the wailing tone used by Indians in songs of sorrow. The tone material is that of a major scale, ending on the tone above the keynote (cf. Nos. 86 and 97). Except for one ascending fifth, the melody progresses by minor thirds and whole tones.

The singer said that, when a child, he heard his father sing the next song. He said that "a man went to the salt water to hunt seal and he saw a seal swimming and heard it sing this song." This is the first song attributed to a seal which has been recorded by the writer, though special inquiry has been made for such songs.

No. 88. Song of a Seal

(Catalog No. 1670)

Recorded by BOB GEORGE

Analysis.—This song contains only the tones of the minor triad and seventh, the latter occurring only as next to the last tone. The transcription is from the first rendition, the subsequent renditions using the same tones and having the same general rhythm, but showing some difference in the order of the phrases. The song consists of two periods of five measures each. Rests occur in these periods, but the rhythmic feeling is carried forward to the end of the phrase.

The preparations for hunting a shark were the same as for hunting whale. (For other songs of this class, see Densmore, 1939.) The weapon used was a spear with a long line, and 8 or 10 canoes joined in the hunt. The shark was killed for its oil, the fat being boiled to secure the oil, which was put in the skin of a seal as a container.

No. 89. Song of a Shark Hunter

(Catalog No. 2062)

Recorded by WILSON WILLIAMS

Voice ♩ = 120
Drum ♩ = 120
Drum rhythm similar to No. 11

Analysis.—The repetition of the phrases in this song is an example of variation in renditions. The song was first sung as transcribed, then the last phrase was sung twice, the first phrase twice, the second phrase five times, and the first phrase twice, the performance being concluded by the end of the phonograph cylinder. Thus there appeared to be no definite number for the repetitions of each phrase. A mannerism which cannot be transcribed consisted in the use of a very short, unaccented tone before each accented tone. The song contains no change of measure length and its chief interest lies in its use and in its simple rhythm.

The man who recorded the next song seems to have a remarkable fluency in expressing himself through music. He said that he once shot and wounded a mountain goat and could not reach the animal, though he tried as hard as he could. That night he thought of the suffering animal and made up this song in which he seems to feel its pain in his own body.

No. 90. Song of a Hunter

(Catalog No. 2030)

Recorded by JIMMIE O'HAMMON

Voice ♩ = 126
Drum ♩ = 126
Drum rhythm similar to No. 14

Free translation.—It hurts where he was shot.

Analysis.—This song is so short that the phonograph cylinder contains many repetitions, without intervening pauses. The rhythmic structure consists of five periods of equal length and the same rhythm, as though a single idea repeated itself in the singer's mind. This is further suggested by the repeated notes with which each phrase begins. The song has a compass of nine tones and contains all the tones of the octave except the fourth.

The rhythm and action of walking, as an inspiration to musical composition, has not previously been noted, but Jimmie O'Hammon said that songs came to him as he "was walking along." (Cf. Densmore, 1939, p. 268.) The next song has no definite use but came to the singer as he walked and was happy.

No. 91. Song of Happiness

(Catalog No. 2029)

Recorded by JIMMIE O'HAMMON

Analysis.—This is a singularly calm and cheerful melody, with a strong individuality. Quadruple measures seldom occur in Indian songs, but there is no secondary accent in the measures thus transcribed in this melody. The tones are those of the fourth 5-toned scale and the song has a compass of 10 tones with a strongly descending trend. Except for 1 interval, the progressions are whole tones and minor thirds.

Pleasant thoughts, as well as the motion of walking, inspired the next song, which is concerning a dream of going to Ottawa.

No. 92. Dream of Going to Ottawa

(Catalog No. 2025)

Recorded by JIMMIE O'HAMMON

Analysis.—The first part of this song, containing the rhythmic unit, is in the upper part of the compass, while the second part, in the lower register, is more determined in rhythm but contains no rhythmic unit. The song has a compass of nine tones and is based on the fourth 5-toned scale.

The singer of this and the song next following is Mrs. Sophie Wilson (pl. 9, fig. 2), who lives at Church House on the Homalco Reserve, north of Butte Inlet. She also recorded a lullaby (No. 77). This is said to be a very old song, the meaning of the words being indicated in the title.

No. 93. "I Wish I Was in Butte Inlet"

(Catalog No. 1678)

Recorded by SOPHIE WILSON

Analysis.—The prominence of ascending intervals, especially in the opening measures, seems to express a yearning, though it is not claimed that the Indian form of expression is similar to that of the white race. The song contains three sorts of ascending and only two sorts of descending intervals. The keynote (A flat) occurs only twice, and one of these occurrences is on the last count of a measure. Attention is directed to a comparison between the rhythmic units, a quarter note being unaccented in the first and accented in the second unit. There is an interesting determination in the rhythm of the closing measures.

Many Indians living on the west coast of British Columbia are employed in the salmon canneries. It appears that the present singer has been a traveler, and it is probable that she has been thus employed. She has pleasant memories of several towns, and also mentions her home, Church House, among the "happy places."

No. 94. Song of a Traveler

(Catalog No. 1679)

Recorded by SOPHIE WILSON

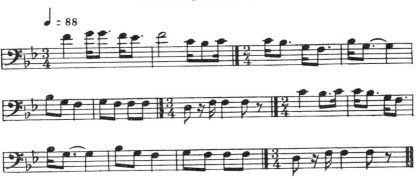

Free translation.—Ridden Cannery is a happy place, they have electric lights; Swell Cove is a happy place, and Tabishin and Church House.

Analysis.—This song was recorded on two entire cylinders, the melody being the same throughout the performance. As first recorded, the melody was said to be a "wihsky song," the words here presented being sung with the second rendition. The song has a compass of 11 tones and is based on the first 5-toned scale in which the third and seventh above the keynote are absent. Thirty of the thirty-four intervals are whole tones and minor thirds.

The next was said to be a "general song" addressed by a man to his niece whose hair was long and handsome. This is the only song recorded by this singer.

No. 95. "Your Pretty Hair"

(Catalog No. 2060)

Recorded by JULIA MALWER

Free translation.—There is nothing that I wish more than your pretty hair, my niece.

Analysis.—The principal part of this melody is on the upper tones of its compass, which is unusual. The descending trend is gradual and the lowest tone occurs only in the final measures. Except for one ascending fifth, the intervals are minor thirds and whole tones. The tone material is the fourth (major) 5-toned (Gaelic) scale and the melody, though strongly individual, suggests the influence of Scotch or Irish melodies.

Next is presented the song of a woman "who longed for happiness, but could not be happy without whiskey."

No. 96. A Woman's Song

(Catalog No. 2043)

Recorded by DENNIS PETERS

Voice ♩ = 60
Drum ♩ = 60
Drum rhythm similar to No. 14

Analysis.—There is an appealing quality in the ascending and descending fourths with which this song opens. A similar song recorded among the Chippewa (Densmore, 1910, No. 137) contains the words "I do not care for you any more." The latter portion of this melody is based on the tonic triad with the fifth as its lowest tone, the song ascending and descending on these tones. With two exceptions the intervals are fourths and whole tones.

There is an element of humor in the next song, which was said to be very old. It is the song of a man, left at home alone, who sings about his wife and wishes she would return.

No. 97. Song of a Man Alone at Home

(Catalog No. 2022)

Recorded by JIMMIE O'HAMMON

Voice   ♩ = 72

Free translation.—Don't be away too long.   Don't stay away if you are not doing anything.

Analysis.—This is a whimsical melody with an ascent of a major sixth in its first two progressions and an almost equal number of ascending and descending intervals. Slight differences occur in the renditions, two of which are transcribed. It is interesting to note a teasing quality, which seems to increase during the performance. The song contains the tones of a major scale ending on the tone above the keynote (cf. Nos. 86 and 87).

The next song was said to have been composed at Kamloops, British Columbia, and to be sung by Indian cowboys when riding the range.

No. 98. Indian Cowboy Song

(Catalog No. 2059)

Recorded by ANNIE BOLEM

♩ = 96

Fine

Analysis.—Six consecutive renditions of this song were recorded, the first half of the performance showing a steady rise in pitch. The first rendition began on E flat, the second ended on F natural, and the fourth rendition began on F sharp, this pitch level being continued to the end of the performance. A rise in pitch level has been noted in Indian songs containing a sudden change in register, this occurring chiefly in Pueblo songs. (Cf. Densmore, 1938, pp. 182–183.) The latter portion of this song is in the lower portion of its compass, which necessitates an ascent of an octave to the first tone of the repetition. This may explain the singer's lack of ability to maintain the level of pitch. The dotted quarter note (B flat) occurring about midway through the melody gives vigor to the rhythm. With one exception the phrases have a descending trend. The low range of voice is often found among Indian women.

MISCELLANEOUS NOTES

The following information was supplied by Dennis Peters:

If a girl comes to maturity in July, the headman comes, cooks a salmon, and gives her a little. If this is not done, the salmon go away.

A girl dreamed that she was fishing. She put down her hook twice without success, and the third time she felt something heavy. The lake was clear and deep. She drew up her line and when the object was about 10 feet below the surface she saw it was the shape of a head. She pulled it up, and it was the wooden mask worn later by the headman when he presided at weddings and important events. The masks were all made like this, and were worn with the open mouth on a level with the wearer's eyes.

SUMMARY OF ANALYSES

These songs were recorded by men and women from widely separated localities and the songs are of many types. For that reason a summary must concern itself with varied characteristics, not with a single pattern peculiar to a region.

Four patterns of melodic structure have been observed in more than 2,500 Indian songs, recorded by the present writer. These are (1) a formation on the simplest overtones of a fundamental, generally called a triad formation, (2) a formation based on the interval of a fourth, (3) a typical folk-song structure which will be described, and (4) a period formation. The fourth pattern does not occur in the present series of songs and the first is not prominent. The second pattern of melody has been connected, in certain tribes, with songs of men, birds, or animals in motion, especially with songs concerning birds (cf. Densmore, 1913, pp. 99–101). In many instances, this pattern consists of ascending and descending intervals of a fourth; in others we find an incomplete tetrachord to which the term "tetratone" has been applied (see p. 18);' and in still others we find a complete tetrachord, with the semitone variously placed. This formation was noted with special frequency among the Nootka and Quileute songs recorded at Neah Bay, Wash. Thirty songs in a total of 210 contained this formation, and a list of the titles and uses of these songs does not connect them with the idea of motion nor with birds and animals. It appears as a distinct form. In this connection, it is interesting to note that the tetrachord was the basis of the musical theory of ancient Greece, the term meaning specifically the four strings of the lyre. The outer strings were always tuned to a perfect fourth, an interval expressed by the Greeks, as in modern times, by the acoustic ratio 3 to 4. The inner strings were tuned in a variety of relations to each other and to the outer strings. The musical theory of Europe since the seventeenth century has been based on the triad, in which the interval between the outer tones is a perfect fifth, expressed by the ratio 2 to 3.

In the songs under present analysis there are instances in which the tetrachord is complete, as in No. 27; instances in which it is incomplete, as in No. 13; and songs in which the fourth is prominent in the framework of the melody, without intermediate tones of sufficient frequency to suggest an incomplete tetrachord, as in Nos. 28, 35, 53, 66, and 79. In songs with this formation the relation of the tones to a keynote is not always clear, showing this to be a distinct type of melody formation.

Mention has been made of the triad formation as occurring infrequently in the present series of songs. Two instances of this formation are Nos. 88 and 90. Special attention is directed to a peculiar pattern of melody in which a keynote is clearly implied, but the song ends on the tone above the keynote, preceded by the keynote. This occurs in Nos. 86, 87, and 97. This has been found in only 9 songs in a total of 1,553 under cumulative analyses (Densmore, 1939), 8 of the number being recorded at Neah Bay, and the ninth being a dance song of the Cocopa Indians on the Mexican border. The three songs in the present series having this ending were recorded by Jimmie O'Hammon. No. 86 is concerning the prophet Skilmaha, No. 97 is a whimsical song of a man left alone at home, and No. 87 is a song of the formal termination of the period of mourning for the dead, a custom observed among the Cocopa and Yuma (cf. Densmore, 1932, pp. 41–100). The songs with this ending recorded at Neah Bay comprised the following: Five Makah songs of the Potlatch and the Klokali dance, and one Makah song of a man who stayed at home from war, this being the same whimsical type of song as No. 97 in the present series. One of the Neah Bay songs with this ending was a Clayoquot song to quiet the waves of the sea, and another was a Quileute song used in treating the sick. It will be noted that five are songs of dances in which foreign influence might be embodied, and two are songs of supposedly magic power, which was frequently attributed to strangers. The visit of "Spaniards" to Neah Bay has been noted (Densmore, 1939, p. 7), and the occurrence of these slight coincidences in musical form becomes significant, especially as the high vocal drone was observed among the Papago of southern Arizona and the Quileute, near Neah Bay. (Cf. Densmore, 1929, p. 14; 1939, pp. 25–26.)

The typical folk-song structure, indicated as the third form of structure in Indian songs, is described as follows by A. H. Fox-Strangways, the eminent English authority on this subject, in an article chiefly concerning English folk song. He states,

the folk singer has not only no harmony (in the sense of other notes than the melody), but no feeling for it . . . His "harmony" is in the tune itself; one note of the tune has an affinity for (or an antipathy to) some other; connections are thus formed, and structure is made possible. Shortly, the folk-songster is satisfied with *affinity* between notes, where we must have *consonance* clinching what is past and prophesying what is to come. The nucleus of his scale is three notes a tone apart (F, G, A, for instance) which have this affinity; above and below this are two outliers, C, D, which also have it; beyond those five he takes notes tentatively. [Fox-Strangways, 1935.]

Without pursuing this subject further, we note the preference for whole tone progressions in the fact that, in the cumulative analysis of 1,343 songs, 41 percent of the progressions were whole tones and 4 percent were semitones. This table of analysis was not extended to the Nootka and Quileute songs, as the uniformity of percentages in various tribes appeared to establish the melodic feature under consideration. This stepping from tone to an adjacent tone is distributed all through Indian melodies and is not a striking contrast to our own usage. It becomes evident as a phase of melodic structure, however, when it is unusually prominent, and this was first observed in songs recorded at Neah Bay. In previous songs it had been shown chiefly in songs with a compass of three tones which formed only 4 percent of 1,553 melodies. At Neah Bay this type of melody was a characteristic of the material, in many of these songs the compass being only three tones with the middle tone as the most prominent. The singer appeared to feel that the middle tone was the basis of his melody, stepping thence to the adjacent tone above and below. Two instances of this in the present series are Nos. 9 and 71, the first being an appeal to certain animals by a doctor when treating the sick, and the second being the song of a man in a "foggy place," confused and uncertain where to go. No. 49 consists of the two intervals of a whole tone each, F sharp–G sharp and B–C sharp. Several songs of the present series end with two whole-tone progressions descending to the keynote. Two songs (Nos. 71 and 75) consist of the three tones, the keynote, its second, and third (major tonality), with one additional tone, the former containing the semitone below, and the latter containing a whole tone above this series. One song, No. 70, contains only the keynote and its major second and major third. These melodies resemble certain dancing songs of the Cocopa (cf. Densmore, 1932, Songs Nos. 116–119).

The Indians of British Columbia have been in contact with people from Scotland for many generations and No. 95 suggests Scotch influence. These songs have not been tabulated with reference to the fourth and second 5-toned scales, often designated as the Gaelic scales. A downward glissando at the end of the song, frequently noted at Neah Bay, appears in No. 44.

An interesting phase of rhythm occurs in Nos. 1 and 42. These songs are felt to be in double rhythm and are transcribed in 2–4 time, yet the stress is equal on the first and second counts of the measure in the larger part of the melody. Transcriptions of Indian songs are divided into measures according to the accented tones, yet the accents in Indian singing are not always emphatic. The uneven measure lengths in Indian songs do not represent a jerky, heavy emphasis on certain tones. There is a rhythm of the melody as a whole which is apparent to a student, hearing the phonograph record over and over many times. This is subtle and constitutes a large part of the charm of the song. The uneven lengths of separate measures should be recognized as part of the larger rhythm of the melody as a whole.

The accompanying drum is usually in a steady meter throughout an Indian song. Thus the metronome indication and the rhythm indication at the beginning of a transcription are understood to be maintained during the entire performance. When an important difference appears it is generally transcribed with the drum on a separate staff. This occurs in Nos. 29, 30, and 31 in the present series. These are war songs. An irregular drumbeat was transcribed with 6 songs recorded at Neah Bay, these comprising 1 dream song, 1 song of the Homatsa dance, and 4 songs of the Klukluwatk dance. One song of the northern Ute, a Turkey dance song, was thus transcribed (cf. Densmore, 1922, No. 30). Among the Yuma and Cocopa Indians, 14 songs were thus transcribed. These comprised, among the Yuma, 8 songs of the Deer dance, 3 of the Lightning dance, and 1 of the Bird dance, with 2 songs of the Cocopa Bird dance (cf. Densmore, 1932, Nos. 50, 55, 57, 58, 59, 60, 62, 63, 64, 66, 69, 97, 105, 110). It is not claimed that the songs transcribed with irregular drumbeat are all the songs in which this occurred.

From the foregoing, it appears that the songs recorded in British Columbia bear interesting resemblances to the songs recorded at Neah Bay and on the Mexican border, as well as resemblances to Scotch songs and to the accepted basis of English folk song. The foregoing observations are offered as an aid to further study, not as presenting any hypothesis or theory. They have arisen in the examination of the melodies, which are transcribed, as nearly as is possible, in ordinary musical notation. These observations suggest influences from the east, across Canada, and also from the south, along the coast of the United States.

BIBLIOGRAPHY

CULLIN, STEWART
 1907. Games of the North American Indians. 24th Ann. Rep. Bur. Amer. Ethnol., 1902–03, pp. 1–846.
DENSMORE, FRANCES
 1910. Chippewa music. Bur. Amer. Ethnol. Bull. 45.
 1913. Chippewa music—II. Bur. Amer. Ethnol. Bull. 53.
 1918. Teton Sioux music. Bur. Amer. Ethnol. Bull. 61.
 1922. Northern Ute music. Bur. Amer. Ethnol. Bull. 75.
 1923. Mandan and Hidatsa music. Bur. Amer. Ethnol. Bull. 80.
 1926. Music of the Tule Indians of Panama. Smithsonian Misc. Coll., vol. 77, No. 11.
 1928. Uses of plants by the Chippewa Indians. 44th Ann. Rep. Bur. Amer. Ethnol. 1926–27, pp. 275–397.
 1929. Chippewa customs. Bur. Amer. Ethnol. Bull. 86.
 1929 a. Papago music. Bur. Amer. Ethnol. Bull. 90.
 1929 b. Pawnee music. Bur. Amer. Ethnol. Bull. 93.
 1932. Menominee music. Bur. Amer. Ethnol. Bull. 102.
 1932 a. Yuman and Yaqui music. Bur. Amer. Ethnol. Bull. 110.
 1936. Cheyenne and Arapaho music. Southwest Mus. Pap. No. 10. Los Angeles.
 1937. The Alabama Indians and their music. In Straight Texas. Publ. Texas Folk-Lore Soc., No. 13, pp. 270–293.
 1938. Music of Santo Domingo Pueblo, New Mexico, Southwest Mus. Pap. No. 12. Los Angeles.
 1939. Nootka and Quileute music. Bur. Amer. Ethnol. Bull. 124.
 1942. A search for songs among the Chitimacha Indians in Louisiana. Anthrop. Pap. No. 19, Bur. Amer. Ethnol. Bull. 133.
FOX-STRANGWAYS, ARTHUR HENRY
 1935. The folksong basis. London Observer. January.
HELMHOLTZ, HERMANN LUDWIG FERDINAND VON
 1885. On the sensations of tone as a physiological basis for the theory of music. Trans. by A. J. Ellis, 2d English ed. London.
MOONEY, JAMES
 1896. The Ghost Dance religion. 14th Ann. Rep. Bur. Ethnol., 1892–93, pt. 2, pp. 641–1110.
SWAN, JAMES G.
 1870. The Indians of Cape Flattery, at the entrance to the Strait of Fuca, Washington Territory. Smithsonian Contr. Knowledge, vol. 16, No. 220, pp. i–ix, 1–106.
SWANTON, JOHN R.
 1909. Tlingit myths and texts. Bur. Amer. Ethnol. Bull. 39.
TEIT, JAMES
 1900. The Thompson Indians of British Columbia. Mem. Amer. Mus. Nat. Hist., vol. 2, Anthrop. 1, No. 4.

1. STREET IN HOP-PICKERS' CAMP.

2. TYPICAL DWELLINGS IN HOP-PICKERS' CAMP.

1. COMMUNAL DWELLING IN HOP-PICKERS' CAMP.

2. "RED CROSS SHACK" IN WHICH SONGS WERE RECORDED. CORPORAL (LATER SERGEANT) WITHERS, OF THE ROYAL CANADIAN MOUNTED POLICE, STANDS IN FOREGROUND

1. GROUP OF INDIANS ENGAGED IN BARTER OF CLOTHING.

2. CORNER OF HOP FIELD.

1. Wires Lowered for Removal of Hops.

2. Indians Gathering Hops.

1. Women Gathering Hops.

2. Wires Raised to Original Position After Removal of Hops.

2. TASALT.

1. INDIAN WOMAN AND CHILD.

1. DWELLING (AT RIGHT) OCCUPIED BY TASALT.

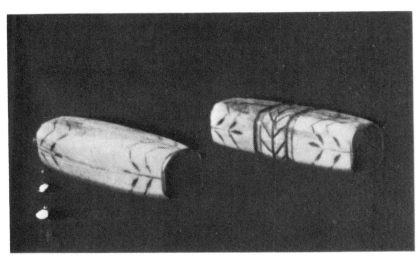

2. BONES USED IN SLAHAL GAME.

1. SLAHAL GAME IN PROGRESS, SHOWING DRUM.

2. SLAHAL GAME IN PROGRESS, LEADER INDICATING "GUESS."

2. MRS. SOPHIE WILSON.

1. HENRY HALDANE.